R.K. Narayan was born in Madras, south India, and educated there and at Maharaja's College in Mysore. His first novel, *Swami and Friends* (1935), and its successor *The Bachelor of Arts* (1937), are both set in the enchanting fictional territory of Malgudi. Other 'Malgudi' novels are: *The Dark Room* (1938), *The English Teacher* (1945), *Mr. Sampath* (1949), *The Financial Expert* (1952), *The Man-Eater of Malgudi* (1961), *The Vendor of Sweets* (1967), *The Painter of Signs* (1977), *A Tiger of Malgudi* (1983), and *Talkative Man* (1986). His novel *The Guide* (1958) won him the National Prize of the Indian Literary Academy, his country's highest literary honour. He was awarded the A.C. Benson Medal in 1980 by the Royal Society of Literature and in 1981 he was made an Honorary Member of the American Academy and Institute of Arts and Letters. In addition to four collections of short stories—*A Horse and Two Goats, An Astrologer's Day and Other Stories, Lawley Road* and *Malgudi Days*—he has published two travel books, *My Dateless Diary* and *The Emerald Route*, two collections of essays, *Next Sunday* and *Reluctant Guru*, and a volume of memoirs, *My Days*. An anthology of his best known works, *Malgudi Landscapes: The Best of R.K. Narayan* was published by Penguin India in 1992.

SALT & SAWDUST

Stories and Table Talk

R.K. NARAYAN

Penguin Books India (P) Ltd., 11 Community Centre, Panchsheel Park, New Delhi 110017 India
Penguin Books Ltd., 27 Wrights Lane, London W8 5TZ, UK
Penguin Putnam Inc., 375 Hudson Street, New York, NY 10014, USA
Penguin Books Australia Ltd., Ringwood, Victoria, Australia
Penguin Books Canada Ltd., 10 Alcorn Avenue, Suite 300, Toronto, Ontario MAV 3B2, Canada
Penguin Books (NZ) Ltd., 182-190 Wairau Road, Auckland 10, New Zealand

First published by Penguin Books India (P) Ltd. 1993

10 9 8 7 6 5

Typeset in New Baskerville by dTech, New Delhi

The author and publishers wish to gratefully acknowledge the following magazines in which these essays first appeared: *Looking for Magsaysay* and *Permitted Laughter* were first published in *The Illustrated Weekly of India*; most of the other essays were first published in *Frontline* (*Teaching in Texas* appeared as *Reluctant Guru* and *Reflections on Frankfurt* as *R.K. Narayan on R.K. Narayan*).

CONTENTS

Foreword vii

SECTION I 1
SALT AND SAWDUST

SECTION II 39
GURU

SECTION III 69
TABLE TALK

Table Talk 71
Looking for Magsaysay 76

Permitted Laughter 116
Reflections on Frankfurt 119
Vayudoot 125
The Enemies 128
On Language 132
Tale of a Tub 135
Teaching in Texas 138
On Walking 145
On Ved Mehta 151
Crowded Day 155
Korean Grass 163
Minister Without Portfolio 167
The Judge 172
Visitor 185
Sampath's Elephant 190
In The Philippines 194
Parrots Ltd. 201
Man-Hunt 213

FOREWORD

A COUPLE OF YEARS AGO, AFTER A BOUT OF illness, I felt that I had written enough fiction and should now undertake lighter work. I could not overcome my impulse to phrase an experience or reaction—the habit of writing dies hard. Sitting down at a certain hour to fill a sheet of paper becomes a conditioned reflex, and I found Table Talk the easiest response.

Table Talk unlike an essay could come to life without too definite a form, on any theme, a few lines without the compulsion of an argument or conclusion, stimulated by a passing scene or mood, or a wisp of an idea floating down from somewhere and vanishing the same way.

I enjoyed writing Table Talk, a term which originated during a casual chat with my friend N. Ram who edits the magazine *Frontline* and who persuaded me to try it. I am indebted to him for not only suggesting it but for also carrying it in the pages of *Frontline* regularly.

Extending the definition of the form, I recently wrote a couple of stories in the same mood: "Salt and Sawdust" and "Guru". The story "Salt and Sawdust" originated from an anecdote narrated by a journalist from Holland. A Dutch lady apparently wrote a laborious bulky novel and sent it to her publisher, who after glancing through it, suggested as a joke, that she would do well to pass her time writing a cookery book. She took him at his word and produced one in the course of time. It became a best-seller and continues in that rank for forty years now.

The other story, "Guru", is based on a miser I know. His devotion to Wealth and the satisfaction he got from watching the rising figures in his bank-book remained his sole joy in life (although it isolated him from his family), and he did not mind the loneliness in a big house, as long as the interest column in his bank-book kept rising.

29 August 1993 — *R.K. Narayan*
Madras

I

SALT AND SAWDUST

ONE

BEING A CHILDLESS COUPLE VEENA AND SWAMI found their one-and-a-half room tenement adequate. A small window opened on Grove Street, a pyol beside the street door served for a sit-out, a kitchen to match, and a backyard with access to a common well. The genius who designed this type of dwelling was Coomar of Boeing Silk Centre, who had bought up an entire row of old houses adjoining his Silk Centre, demolished and rebuilt them to house his staff working in the weaving factory beyond the river. It proved a sound investment and also enabled Coomar to keep his men under his thumb.

Swami left (on his bicycle) for his factory at

seven-thirty a.m. but got up at five, while his wife was still asleep. He drew water from the common well, lit the stove and prepared coffee and lunch for two, packing up a portion to carry. Veena got up late, gulped down the coffee kept on the stove, swept the floor and cleaned the vessels. After her bath, she lit an oil lamp before the image of a god in a niche. After lunch, she sat on the pyol, watched the street, with a magazine in hand, and brooded over a novel she was planning to write, still nebulous.

She felt she could start writing only when she got a proper notebook, which Swami had promised to bring this evening. While returning home Swami stopped by Bari's Stationery Mart on Market Road and announced, 'My wife is going to write a novel. Can you give me a good notebook?'

'How many pages?' Bari asked mechanically. Swami had no idea. He did not want to risk a conjecture.

'Please wait. I'll find out and come back,' he said and tried to leave.

Bari held him back, 'I know what you want. We are supplying notebooks to novelists all the time. Take this home.' He pressed into his hand a brown packet. 'Two hundred pages Hamilton Bond, five rupees. Come back for more—our notebooks are lucky. Many writers have become famous after buying from us.'

Veena was thrilled. She gazed on the green calico binding, flicked the pages, and ran her fingers tenderly over the paper.

'Now I can really start writing. I have been scribbling on slips of paper—old calendar sheets and such things.' She flicked the pages again, and cried, 'Lined too.'

'Lined sheets are a great help. When you want another one, tell me, and I'll get it,' he said.

'I want 400 pages, but this will do for the present,' she was so pleased that she felt she should do him a good turn. She hugged him and asked, 'Shall I cook our dinner tonight?'

'No, no,' he cried desperately.

On earlier occasions when she had cooked he had swallowed each morsel with difficulty, suppressing comment, and silently suffering. He felt that they might have to starve unless he took over the kitchen duties. He realized that she was not made for it. Boiling, baking, spicing, salting, blending, were beyond her understanding or conception. He was a good eater with taste and appetite. 'A novelist probably cannot be a good cook,' he concluded, 'just as I cannot write a novel. She has not been taught to distinguish salt from sawdust.' He quietly took over the kitchen leaving her free to write whatever she fancied.

However, he would enquire from time to time, 'What progress?' She answered, 'Can't say anything now, we have to wait.'

Several days later, when he asked for progress, she said, 'The heroine is just emerging.'

'What do you call her?'

'Oh, names come very last in a novel.'

'In that case, how can a reader know who is who?'

'Just wait and see, it is my responsibility.'

'I could write only two pages today,' she said another day.

'Keep it up. Very soon you will fill four, eight, sixteen pages a day.' His vision soared on multiples of four for some obscure reason. 'I think I had better buy another 200-page notebook before Bari's stock is exhausted. He said that the demand from the novelists is rather heavy this season.'

'Did he mention any novelist's name?'

'I will ask next time.' After that he went into his room to change into a garb to suit his kitchen work. When he came out in a knee-length dhoti and a towel over his shoulder she said, 'I was asking if he had met any novelist.'

'Bari has met any number. I know only one novelist and she stands before me now.' He then asked, 'What kind of a man is your hero?'

She replied, 'What do you imagine him to be?'

'Tall, and powerful, not a fellow to be trifled with.'

'So be it,' she said, and asked, 'is he a fighting sort?'

'Maybe if he is drawn to it . . . .'

She completed his sentence, 'He won't hesitate to knock off the front teeth of anyone—'

Swami found the image of an adversary minus his teeth amusing, and asked, 'What about the rest of his teeth?'

'He will deal with them when he is challenged next.'

'You almost make him a dentist,' he said.

'A Chinese dentist has opened a clinic at New

Extension, and a lot of people sit before him open-mouthed.'

'How have you come to know about it?'

'Sometimes I lock the door and wander about till it is time to return home. Otherwise I cannot get ideas.'

'When will you find time to write if you are wandering about?'

'Wandering about is part of a writer's day. I also carry a small book and jot down things that interest me.'

'Excellent plan,' he said and disappeared into the kitchen as he smelt burning oil from the frying pan.

TWO

VEENA DEVELOPED THE IDEA FURTHER, AND said, when they settled down on the hall-bench after supper, 'I think a Chinese dentist is the hero, it is something original, no one has thought of him before. Chinese dentists are famous.'

'But how can a girl of our part of the world marry a Chinese?'

'Why not?' she said and thought it over and said, 'In the novel actually he is not a Chinese. He had only his training in China.'

'Why did he go to China?' asked Swami.

'When he was a boy he ran away from home.'

'Why?'

'His schoolmaster caned him one day and, in

sheer disgust, he went and slept on a bench at the railway platform for two days and nights. When a train passed at midnight, he slipped into a carriage and finally joined some monks and sailed for Peking in a boat.'

'Very interesting, very interesting,' Swami cried. 'How do you get these ideas?'

'When one writes, one gets ideas,' she explained, and continued, 'the monks left him at the port and vanished . . . .'

'Were they supernatural beings? Could you explain their presence and help?'

'God must have sent them down to help the boy . . . .'

'Why should God be interested?' Swami asked.

'God's ways are mysterious.'

'True, God's ways are certainly mysterious,' he endorsed her philosophy. She continued, 'And the young fellow wandered here and there in the streets of Peking, without food or shelter for a couple of days, and fainted in front of a dentist's clinic. In the morning when the dentist came to open the door, he saw the boy and thought he was dead.'

'What do they do in China with the dead?' he asked in genuine concern and added, 'they probably bury . . . .'

'No, no, if he was buried that would end my story,' she said. 'The Chinese are probably careful and cautious, unlike in our country, where they immediately carry away a body and dispose of it.'

'Not that way,' Swami said, showing off his better

knowledge of the situation. 'Once when I was working in a cloth shop, a body was found in the veranda and they immediately sent for a doctor.'

'Why a doctor when he or she is already dead?'

'That's a routine in such circumstances—' he generalized.

'I want you to find out from someone what the Chinese do when a body is found at the door. I must know before I proceed with the story.'

He said, 'Since he becomes the Chinese dentist of your story later, he was not really dead—so why bother about it?'

'Of course,' she agreed. 'When he came back home, he knew how to work as a dentist, and became prosperous and famous.'

'Readers will question you . . . .'

'Oh, leave that to me, it is my business.'

The story was taken one step further at the next conference. They had both got into the habit of talking about it every evening after dinner, and were becoming, unconsciously, collaborators.

'He fell in love with a girl, who had somehow lost all her teeth and come to fit new ones . . . . Day by day as he saw her with her jaws open to be fitted up, he began to love her, being physically so close to each other . . . .'

Veena gloated over the vision of love blossoming in a dentist's chair . . . .

Swami became critical, 'With her jaws open, toothless gums, do you think it is possible for a man to be attracted? Any romance possible in that state?'

'Don't you know that love is blind?'

Not wanting to appear to cross-examine or discourage her, he said, 'Ah, now I understand, it is natural that a man who bends so close over a woman's face cannot help it, and it's his chance to whisper in her ears his passion though if a toothless person comes before me, I would not care for her.' Veena took offence at this point.

'So that means if I lose my teeth, you will desert me?'

'No, no, you will always be my darling wife. But all that I am trying to say is, when the teeth are lost both the cheeks get sucked in and the mouth becomes pouchy, and the whole face loses shape.'

She was upset at this remark, got up and went away to the corner where her books were kept and started reading, ignoring him.

By the time they sat down again next night after dinner, she relented enough to say, 'He need not be a dentist—I agree it's an awkward situation for lovers . . . . Shall I say that he is something in a less awkward profession, a silk merchant or a veterinary doctor?'

Swami was pleased that she had conceded his point, and felt that it was now his turn to concede a point and said, 'No, no, let him be what he is, it's very original, don't change—this is probably the first time a dentist comes into a story . . . .'

And on that agreeable note, peace was established once again. The dentist had to work on the heroine's gums for a long time taking moulds and preparing her dentures, trying them out, filing, fitting and bridging. All the time Cupid was at work. It took the dentist several weeks to complete his task and beautify her face. When it was accomplished he proposed and they married, overcoming obstacles.

THREE

As the notebook was getting filled, Veena took an afternoon off to spend time at the Town Hall Library, to browse through popular magazines on the hall table and romances in the shelves, desperately seeking ideas. Not a single book in the whole library on the theme of a dentist and a bare-gummed heroine. She returned home and remained silent all through the evening, leaving Swami to concentrate on his duties in the kitchen. She sat in her corner trying to go on with the story until Swami called from the kitchen, 'Dinner ready.'

One evening she confessed: 'I have not been able to write even two lines today. I don't know in which language I should continue.' She was suddenly facing a problem. She was good in English—always remembered her 60 per cent in English literature in BA. At the same time she felt she could write in Tamil, and felt it her duty to enrich her mother tongue, so that all classes of people could benefit from her writing. It was an inner struggle, which she did not reveal even to her husband, but he sensed something was wrong and enquired tactfully, 'Want anything?'

'What is our language?' she asked.

'Tamil, of course.'

'What was the language of my studies at Albert Mission?'

'English.'

'How did I fare in it?'

'You always got 60 per cent.'

'Why should I not write in English?'

'Nobody said you should not.'

'But my conscience dictates I should write only in my mother tongue.'

'Yes, of course,' he agreed.

'You go on saying "Yes" to everything. You are not helping me.' He uttered some vague mumbling sounds.

'What are you trying to say?' she asked angrily. He remained silent like a schoolboy before an aggressive pedagogue.

'Don't you realize that English will make my novel known all over India if not the whole world?'

'Very true,' he said with a forced smile. 'Why is she grilling me?' he reflected. 'After all, I know nothing about writing novels. I am only a weaving supervisor at Coomar's factory.' He said to himself further, 'Anyway, it's her business. No one compels her to write a novel. Let her throw it away. If she finds time hanging heavily, let her spin yarn on a charka.' He suddenly asked, 'Shall I get you a charka?'

'Why?' she asked rather alarmed at his irrelevancy.

'Mahatma Gandhi had advised every citizen of India to spin as a patriotic duty. They are distributing charkas almost free at Gandhi Centre . . . .' By this time she felt that something was amiss, abruptly got up and went over to her canvas chair in the corner, picking up a book from her cupboard. He sat in his wooden chair without moving or speaking. He began to feel that silence would be the safest course, fearing, as in a law court, any word he uttered might be used against him. He sat looking out of the window though nothing was happening there, except a donkey swishing its tail under the street lamp, 'Flies are bothering it,' he observed to himself, 'otherwise it could be the happiest donkey.' His neighbour was returning home with a green plastic bag filled with vegetables and passed by with a nod. Swami found the silence oppressive, and tried to break it, 'Mahatma Gandhi had advised that every individual should spin morning and evening and that'd solve a lot of problems.'

'What sort of problems?' she asked gruffly looking up from her book.

He answered, 'Well, all sorts of problems people face,' he replied from his seat.

'What makes you talk of that subject now?' She was too logical and serious, he commented within himself, 'Has to be. Novelists are probably like that everywhere.' He remained silent not knowing how to proceed or in which direction. She sued for peace two days later by an abrupt announcement, 'Have decided to write both in Tamil and English, without bothering about the language just as it comes. Sometimes I think in English, sometimes in Tamil, ideas are more important than language. I'll put down the ideas as they occur to me, if in English, it'll be English, if the next paragraph comes in Tamil I'll not hesitate to continue in Tamil, no hard and fast rule.'

'Of course there should be no hard and fast rules in such matters. To be reduced to a single language in the final stage, I suppose?'

'Why should I?' she said slightly irritated. 'Don't we mix English and Tamil in conversation?'

He wanted to say, 'If you knew Hindi, you could continue a few paragraphs in Hindi too, it being our national language as desired by Mahatma Gandhi,' but he had the wisdom to suppress it. Another mention of Gandhi might destroy the slender fabric of peace, but he asked solicitously, 'Will you need another book for writing?'

'Yes,' she said, 'I am abandoning this notebook, and will make a fresh start on a new notebook . . . .' His mind got busy planning what to do with the blank pages of the present notebook. 'I don't want to look at those pages again. I'll start afresh. You may do what you please with this notebook. Get me another one without fail tomorrow . . . .'

'Perhaps you may require two books, if you are writing in two languages, it may prove longer.'

'Difficult to say anything about it now, but bring me one book that will do for the present . . . .'

'I will tell Bari to keep one in reserve in any case . . . .' he said. It went on like that. It became a routine for her to fill her notebook, adding to the story each day. They used to talk about it, until one day she announced, 'They are married. It is a grand wedding since he was a popular dentist, and a lot of people in the town owed their good looks to him. His clinic was expanded and he engaged several assistants, and he was able to give his wife a car and a big house, and he had a farm outside the city, and they often spent their weekends at the farm.'

'Any children?'

'By and by, inevitably.'

'How many are you going to give him?'

'We will see,' she said, and added, 'at some point I must decide whether to limit their offspring to one or several.'

'But China has the highest population,' he said.

'True, but he is not a real Chinese, he only trained there,' she said, correcting him.

He said, 'Then he must have at least four children. Two sons and two daughters, the first and the third must be daughters.' He noticed that she looked annoyed . . . too much interference she suddenly felt, and lapsed into silence.

'Suppose they also have twins?' he dared.

'We can't burden them that way having no knowledge of bringing up a child ourselves.'

'God will give us children at the appointed time . . . .'

'But you assume that we could recklessly burden the couple in the story!' she said.

FOUR

VEENA WROTE STEADILY, FILLED UP PAGE AFTER page of a fresh notebook . . . and with a look of triumph told Swami, 'I won't need another notebook . . . .' She held up the notebook proudly. He looked through the pages, shook his head in appreciation of her feat in completing the work; not entirely her work, he had a slight share in her accomplishment, of the 200 pages in the book he had contributed ten pages, and was proud of it. In the story, at the dentist's wedding, an elaborate feeding programme was described for a thousand guests. The feast was very well-planned—two days running they served breakfast, coffee and idli and dosai and uppuma and two sweets and fruit preparations, a heavy lunch with six vegetables and rice preparations, concluding with a light elegant supper. Fried almonds and nuts were available in bowls all over the place, all through the day. The bridegroom, the dentist, had expressed a wish that a variety of eatables must be available for those with weak teeth or even no teeth, he had all kinds of patients, capable of different degrees of chewing and mastication.

Food had to be provided for them in different densities and calibre. Arrangements were made not only to provide for those who could chew hardstuff, masticate a stone with confidence, but also for those who could only swallow a mashed, over-ripe banana. The doctor was saying again and again, 'It is my principle that a marriage feast must be remembered—not only by those endowed with thirty-two teeth, but also by the unfortunate ones who have less or none.' At this stage Swami and Veena lost sight of the fact that it was a piece of fiction that they were engaged in and went on to chart every meal with tremendous zest. Swami would brook no compromise: it had to be the finest cuisine in every aspect. 'Why should you make it so elaborate and gluttonous?' Veena asked.

He answered, 'The guests should have a wide choice, let them take it or leave it. Why should we bother? Anyway, it is to cost us nothing. Why not make it memorable?' So he let himself go. He explained what basic ingredients were required for the special items in the menu, the right stores which supplied only clean grains and pulses imported from Tanjore and Sholapur, honey and saffron from Kashmir, apples from Kulu valley, and rose water from Hyderabad to flavour sherbets to quench the afternoon thirst of guests, spices, cardamom, cinnamon and cloves from Kerala, and chillies and tamarind from Guntur . . . . Swami not only knew where to get the best, but also how to process, dry, grind, and pulverize them before cooking. He also knew how to make a variety of sun-dried fritters, wafers and chips. He arranged for sesame from somewhere to extract the best frying oil, butter from somewhere else to melt and obtain fragrant ghee. He wrote down everything including detailed recipes on the blank pages of the notebook that Veena had abandoned. When he presented his composition to Veena, she said, 'Too long, I'll take only what is relevant to my story.' She accepted only ten pages of his writing, rewrote it, and blended it into her narrative—even with that Swami felt proud of his participation in a literary work.

Swami took the completed novel to Bari, who looked through the pages and said, 'The lady, your missus, must be very clever.'

'Yes, she is,' said Swami, 'otherwise how could one write so much? I could only help her with ideas, now and then, but I am no writer.'

Bari said, 'I can't read your language or English very much, but I'll show it to a scholar I know, who buys paper and stationery from me. He is a professor in our college—a master of eighteen languages.'

It took ten days to get an opinion. Ten days of suspense for Veena, who constantly questioned Swami at their night sessions after dinner, 'Suppose the professor says it is no good?' Swami had to reassure again and again, 'Don't worry. He'll like it. If he doesn't, we will show it to another scholar . . . .' Every evening he stopped by at Bari's to ask for the verdict, while Veena waited anxiously for Swami's return.

'Wait, wait, don't be nervous. Scholars will take their own time to study any piece of work. We can't rush them . . . .'

One evening he brought her the good news. The scholar's verdict was favourable. He approved especially the double language experiment which showed originality. Veena could not sleep peacefully that night, nor let her husband sleep, agitated by dreams of success and fame as a novelist.

She disturbed him through the night in order to discuss the next step. 'Should we not find a publisher in Madras? They know how to reach the readers.'

'Yes, yes,' he muttered sleepily.

'We may have to travel to Madras . . . . Can you take leave? If Coomar refuses to let you go, you must resign. If the novel is taken, we may not have to depend upon Coomar. If it becomes a hit, film-makers will come after us, that'll mean . . . .' Her dreams soared higher and higher. Swami was so frequently shaken out of sleep that he wondered why he should not take a pillow and move to the pyol outside.

Bari stopped their plan to visit Madras. 'Why should you go so far for this purpose? I have paper and a friend has the best press . . . .'

'Where?' asked Swami.

'You know Mango Lane, just at the start of Mempi Hill Road.'

'No, never been there . . . .'

'Once it was an orchard, where mangoes were cultivated and exported to Europe and America, till my friend bought the place, cleared the grove, and installed a press there. He prints and publishes many books, also for the government, reports and railway time-tables. I supply all the paper he needs, a good customer—not always for our Hamilton Brand but he buys all sorts. His name is Natesh, a good friend, he will print anything I want. Why should you wait upon publishers in Madras? They may not accept the novel, having their own notions, or if they take it, they may delay for years. I know novelists who have aged while waiting and waiting.'

'Impossible to wait,' said Swami recollecting his wife's anxiety and impatience to see herself in print.

FIVE

BARI HAD THE PRINTER WAITING AT HIS SHOP. He told Swami, 'My friend came to order some thin paper for handbills, and I have held him back.' Natesh was a tall, lean, bearded person who wore a khadi kurta and dhoti, forehead smeared with vermilion and holy ash. Natesh wished to see the manuscript. Swami produced the notebook for the printer's inspection next day. But when he suggested he take it with him to Mango Lane, for estimating the printing charges, Swami felt embarrassed, not being sure if Veena would like to let it out of sight. He said, 'I'll bring it back later, the author is still revising it.' Natesh went through the pages, counting the lines for about fifteen minutes, noting down the number of lines and pages, and declared, 'I'll give an estimate for printing and binding in two days.'

'I'll give an estimate for the paper required—that's my business,' added Bari. On this hopeful note they parted for the evening.

Coming to brass tacks a couple of days later, Bari made a proposal: 'I'll supply the paper definitely as your friend, Natesh, has calculated that you will need twenty reams of white printing for the text, extra for covers. We will print 500 copies at first. It would have cost less if the text had been in a single language but now the labour charges are more for two languages, and Natesh wants to print Tamil in black ink and English in red ink on a page, and that'll also cost more. I can supply printing ink also. It would have been cheaper if your missus had written less number of pages and in her mother tongue only.' Swami said, being ignorant of the intricacies of the creative process, 'I will tell her so.'

'No, no,' cried Bari in alarm. 'I'd not like to offend her, sir . . . . Novelists must be respected, and must be left to write in as many languages they choose, who are we to question?'

The printer at their next meeting said, 'I can give a rough estimate, not the final one unless I go through the text for two days, and I won't undertake printing without going through the text to assure myself that it contains no blasphemy, treason, obscenity or plagiarism. It's a legal requirement, if there is any of the above I'll be hauled up before a magistrate . . . . ' Swami became panicky, he had not read the manuscript (but even if he had) he could not say what offences Veena might have committed, but protested aloud, 'Oh, no! Bari knows me and my family, and our reputation . . . .' Bari endorsed this sentiment, 'Such offences are unthinkable in their family, they are very well-known, high class, otherwise they can't be my customers: I would not sell Hamilton Bond paper to anyone and everyone unless I am convinced that they are lawful persons belonging to good families. If I gave my best paper to all and sundry, where would I be?' Swami had no answer to this question as he could not follow the logic of Bari's train of thought. They were sitting around on low aluminium stools and Swami's back ached, sitting erect and stiff on a circular seat which had neither an armrest nor a back. He stood up. Bari cried, 'Sit, down, sit down. You must have tea.' He beckoned his servant, an urchin he had brought with him from Aligarh, whom he never let out of sight. 'Jiddu, three cups of tea. Tell that man to give the best tea, otherwise I'll not pay . . . .' While the boy dashed out for tea, Natesh said, 'Apart from other things I must guard against plagiarism.' Swami had heard of plague, but not plagiarism. 'Please explain,' he said. When Natesh explained, he grew panicky. He wondered if his wife visited the Town Hall library to lift passages from other books. As soon as he went home, he asked his wife, 'Did you go to the Town Hall library?'

'Not today . . . .'

'But when you go there what do you generally do?'

'Why this sudden interest?' she asked. He retreated into his shell again, 'Just wanted to know if you found any story as good as yours in the library . . . .' She brushed off his enquiry with a gesture.

He coaxed and persuaded her to give the novel for the printer's inspection next day. With many warnings she let him take the notebook away with him, expressing her own doubt, 'If he copies and sells it?'

'Oh, no, he can't do it. We will hand him over to the police, if he does it. Bari will be our witness. We'll take a receipt.'

Next day at Bari's, Swami met Natesh and handed him the notebook.

Six

NATESH TOOK THREE DAYS TO COMPLETE HIS scrutiny of the novel and brought back the manuscript, safely wrapped in brown paper, along with the estimate. They conferred once again behind a stack of paper. There was silence while Jiddu was gone to fetch three cups of tea. After drinking tea Bari said, 'Let us not waste time. Natesh, have you the estimate ready?'

'Here it is,' said Natesh holding out a long envelope, Bari received it and passed it on to Swami with a flourish. Then he asked the printer, 'How do you find the novel?'

'We will talk about it later—'

Bari said, 'If you are not interested, Swami's missus

will take it to the Madras printers.'

'Why should she?' asked Natesh, 'While we are here?'

'If so, come to the point. I'll supply the paper at less than cost price, when the book is sold you may pay . . . .'

Swami felt rather disturbed. 'But you said the other day, you would supply it . . . .'

Bari said, 'I am a business man, sir, I only said I'd supply, I meant I would supply, nothing more and nothing less . . . .'

At this point Natesh said, 'You have not seen my estimate yet. Why don't you look through it first . . . .' Swami felt he was being crushed between heavy-weights. He opened the estimate, took a brief look at the bewildering items, and then at the bottom line giving the total charges, felt dizzy, abruptly got up and rushed out into the street without a word, leaving the two agape.

Veena was standing at the door as usual. Even at a distance she could sense that something had gone wrong, judging from Swami's gait and downcast eyes. When he arrived and passed in without a word, she felt a lump in her throat. Why was he uncommunicative today? Normally he would greet her while coming up the steps. Today he was silent, could it be that the printer had detected some serious lapse, moral or legal, in her novel and threatened him with action? They ate in silence. When they settled down in their seats in the front room, she ventured to ask, 'What happened?'

'Nothing,' he said. 'I have brought back the book.'

'I see it. Are they not going to print it?'

'No, unless we sell ourselves and all that we have, to pay their bill. Even Bari has proved tricky and backed out though he had almost promised to supply the paper.'

He went over to his cupboard and brought out the estimate. Veena studied it with minute attention, tried to understand the items in the bill, then let out a deep sigh, and showed symptoms of breaking down. Immediately Swami shed his gloom, assumed a tone of reckless cheer and said, 'You should not mind these setbacks, they are incidental in the career of any writer. I do not know very much about these things, but I have heard of authors facing disappointments all through life until a sudden break of good fortune occurred, even Shakespeare, you are a first class literary student and you must have read how downhearted he was till his plays were recognized.'

'Who told you? I have never seen you read Shakespeare.' This piece of conversation, however, diverted her attention, and she said overcoming her grief, 'Let us go away to Madras, where we will find the right persons to appreciate the novel. This is a wretched town. We should leave it.' He felt happy to see her spirit revive, secretly wondering if she was going to force him to lose his job. Without contradicting her, he just murmured, 'Perhaps we should write to the publishers and ask them first.'

'No,' she said, 'it will be no use. Nothing can be done through letters. It will be a waste of time and money . . . .' He felt an impulse to ask, 'On reaching Madras are you going to stand outside the railway station and cry out, "I have arrived with my novel, who is buying it?" Will publishers come tumbling over each other to snatch up your notebook?' He suppressed his thoughts as usual.

She watched him for a while and asked, 'What do you think?'

'I'll see Coomar and ask him for a week off . . . .'

'If he refuses, you must resign and come out . . . .' This was the second time she was toying with the idea of making him jobless, little realizing how they were dependent on Coomar for shelter and food. Somehow she had constituted herself Coomar's foe. This was not the time to argue with her. He merely said, 'Coomar will understand, but this is a busy production season, lot of pressure at the moment.'

She grumbled, 'He wants to make more money, that is all, he is not concerned with other people's interests. That is all . . . .' Swami felt distressed at her notion of his boss, whom he respected. He swallowed his words and remained silent.

SEVEN

SOME DAYS LATER, ONE AFTERNOON THEY WERE visited by Bari and Natesh. It was a holiday and Swami was at home. He became fussy and drew the available furniture here and there, dashed next door and borrowed a folding chair, and managed seats for everybody. Veena threw a brief glance at the visitors, and walked past them unceremoniously and was off, while Swami fell into a state of confusion, torn between surprise at the arrival of visitors and an impulse to go after Veena. His eyes constantly wandered to the corner of the street while greeting and welcoming his visitors. 'Your missus going out in a hurry?' asked Bari.

'Yes, yes, she has an engagement in Fourth Lane, busy all day . . . .'

'Writing all the time?' asked the bearded man, whose bulging eyes and forehead splashed with holy ash and vermilion gave him a forbidding look. 'Yes, yes, she has to answer so many letters everyday from publishers in Madras . . . before we go there . . . .' The two guests looked at each other in consternation.

'No need, no need,' they cried in unison, 'while we are here . . . .'

'But she has definite plans to take her novel to Madras . . . .' Swami said. When they said, 'No, sir, please, she will bring fame to Malgudi . . . .' Swami felt emboldened by their importunity, and said in a firm tone, 'Your charges for printing will make me bankrupt and a beggar . . . .' He looked righteous.

'But, sir, it was only a formality, estimates are only a business formality. You must not take it to heart, estimates are provisional and negotiable . . . .'

'Why did you not say so?' asked Swami authoritatively. He felt free to be rude.

'But you went away before we could say anything.' Swami gave a fitting reply as he imagined. Veena's absence gave him freedom. She would have controlled him with a look or by a thought wave, as he sometimes suspected, whenever a third person was present. He realized suddenly his social obligations, 'May I offer you tea or coffee?'

After coffee and the courtesies, they came down to business. Natesh suddenly said: 'I was in prison during the political struggle for independence, and being a political sufferer our government gave me a pension, and all help to start my printing press—I always remind myself of Mahatmaji's words and conduct myself in all matters according to his commands . . . .' He doubtless looked like one in constant traffic with the other world to maintain contact with his Master. 'Why am I saying this to you now?' he suddenly asked. Bari had the answer for it, 'To prove that you will always do your best and that you are a man of truth and non-violence.' The other smiled in satisfaction, and then remarked, 'Your wife has gone out, and yet you have managed to give us coffee, such good coffee!'

'Oh, that's no trouble. She keeps things ready at all times. I leave her as much time as possible for her writing too.' They complimented him on his attitude and domestic philosophy. Bari said, 'We will not allow the novel to go out, we will do it here.'

The other said, 'I am no scholar or professor, but I read the story and found it interesting, and in some places I was in tears when the young couple faced obstacles. I rejoiced when they married . . . . Don't you think so?' he asked turning to Bari.

'Alas, I am ignorant of the language. If it had been in our language I'd have brought it out famously, but you have told me everything, and so I feel I have read it. Yes, it is a very moving story, I'll supply the paper and Natesh will print it . . . .'

'Where?' asked Swami.

'In my press of course. At Madras I learnt the ins

and outs of the publishing business. Under the British, publishers were persecuted, especially, when we brought out patriotic literature, and then I had to give up my job when Mahatmaji ordered individual Satyagraha .... I was arrested for burning the Union Jack, and went to prison. After I was released, the Nehru government helped us to start life again. But now I am concentrating on printing ... but if I find a good author, I am prepared to publish his work. I know how to market any book which seems good.'

'So you think this novel will sell?' asked Swami buoyed up. 'Yes, by and by, I know when it should be brought out. In this case the novel should be published later as a second book, we will keep it by. Your story portion stands by itself, but without spoiling it we can extract the other portion describing the marriage feast as a separate part, and publish it as the first book, with a little elaboration—perhaps adding more recipes of the items served in the feast—it can then become a best seller. While reading it, my mouth watered and I felt hungry. It's so successfully presented. With a little elaboration it can be produced as a separate book and will definitely appeal to the reader, sort of an appetizer for the book to follow, that's the novel, readers will race for it when they know that the feast will again be found in the novel. If you accept the idea we may immediately proceed. I know how to sell it all over the country. The author is at her best in describing food and feast. If you can give me a full book on food and feast, I can give you an agreement immediately. On signing it, I'll give you one thousand and one thousand on publication. We will bring it out at our own cost. When it sells, we will give you a royalty of 10 per cent, less the advance.'

Later Swami explained the offer to Veena. Veena immediately said dolefully, 'They want a cookery book, and not a novel.'

'I think so,' Swami said. 'But he will give a thousand rupees if you agree. Imagine one thousand, you may do many things . . . .'

'But the novel?'

'He will publish it as a second book, after your name becomes known widely with the first book.'

'But I don't know any cookery . . . .'

'It doesn't matter, I will help you . . . .'

'You have never allowed me in the kitchen . . . .'

'That should make no difference. You will learn about it in no time and become an authority on the subject . . . .'

'Are you making fun of me?'

'Oh, no. You are a writer. You can write on any subject under the sun. Wait a minute.' He went up to a little trunk in which he kept his papers, brought out the first green-bound notebook in which he had scribbled notes for the dentist's marriage feast. Veena went through it now carefully, and asked, 'What do you want me to do?'

'You must rewrite each page of my notes in your own words—treat it as a basis for a book on the subject . . . .'

'What about the novel?'

'That will follow, when you have a ready-made public . . . .' She sat silently poring over the pages which she had earlier rejected, but now found the contents absorbing. She thought over it and shook him again that night while he was sound asleep, and said, 'Get me a new notebook tomorrow. I'll try.'

Next evening on his way home, Swami picked up a Hamilton notebook. Veena received it quietly. Swami left it at that till she herself said after three days, 'I'll give it a trial first . . . .'

That afternoon, after lunch she sat in her easy chair, and wrote a few lines, the opening lines being: 'After air and water, man survives by eating, all of us know how to eat, but not how to make what one eats.' She wrote in the same tone for a few pages and explained that the pages following were planned to make even the dull-witted man or woman an expert cook . . . . She read it out to Swami that evening. He cried, 'Wonderful, all along I knew you could do it, all that you have to do now is to elaborate the points from my notes in your own style, and that'll make a full book easily . . . .'

Swami signed a contract on behalf of Veena, received Rs 1,000 advance in cash.Veena completed her task in three months and received Rs 1,000 due on delivery of the manuscript. Natesh was as good as his word and Bari supplied the best white printing paper at concessional rates. They called the book: *Appetizer—A Guide to Good Eating.* Natesh through his contacts with booksellers sold out the first edition of

2,000 copies within six months. It went through several editions and then was translated into English and several Indian languages, and Veena became famous. She received invitations from various organizations to lecture and demonstrate. Swami drafted her speeches on food subjects, travelled with her, and answered questions at meetings. They were able to move out of Grove Street to a bungalow in New Extension, and Veena realized her long-standing desire to see her husband out of Coomar's service. All his time was needed to look after Veena's business interests and the swelling correspondence, mostly requests for further recipes, and advice on minor problems in the kitchen. Though he offered to continue cooking their meals, Veena prohibited him from stepping into the kitchen, and engaged a master cook. In all this activity the novel was not exactly forgotten, but awaited publication. Natesh always promised to take it up next, as soon as the press was free, but *Appetizer* reprints kept the machines overworked, and there was no sign of the demand slackening. Veena, however, never lost hope of seeing her novel in print and Swami never lost hope that some day he would be allowed to cook; and the master cook could be secretly persuaded or bribed to leave.

II

GURU

ALL ALONE IN A BIG HOUSE, HE FELL PREY TO A jumble of thoughts as he sat at the window overlooking Vinayak Street. Reclining in his ancient canvas chair, he gazed ahead at nothing in particular, an old rain-tree on which were assembled crows of the locality, passing clouds, bullock carts, cyclists, and uninteresting passers-by. His wife had left him months ago, his two daughters seemed to have abandoned him too. His first daughter, Raji, the best of the lot, was in Trichy and his second in Lawley Extension only a couple of miles away but as far as he was concerned she might be in Mars or the Moon, displaying an indifference which was inhuman.

I am past sixty and feel orphaned, though, I slaved all my life to bring up the family . . . I have no craving for their company. Only, I want them to realize that I do not need anyone's help, strong enough still, thank God, to look after myself. That Pankaja Lodge man sends me food in a brass container for four rupees a meal, enough quantity for two and I save a portion for the night too . . . if I feel hungry in between, a bun from the shop across the street costs only ten paise each. In all, I do not have to spend more than Rs 150 a month, whereas my wife used to demand 1,000 for housekeeping! I am surviving much to their surprise, a tiny portion of the self-generating interest from my savings is more than enough to keep me alive. And then the rent from the shops on Grove Street. Assets built up laboriously, risking my reputation and job.

My family never cared to understand. How I wish they were appreciative and grateful! God is my only ally, He will never forsake me, I need no one else. I get up at six in the morning, bathe and worship the images in the puja room, read the *Ramayana* all afternoon. (I am not the sort to sleep in the afternoon.) I feel elated when I hold that ancient volume in my hand, the only treasure that could be named my ancestral property, which my brother claimed and gave up since I firmly told him that I would not tear out its pages in order to provide him a share; and in compensation he grabbed a copper bowl, a deer skin on which my father used to sit and meditate, and a bamboo staff.

I tell God, first thing in the day and again at night before sleep overcomes me, 'Sir, you have been extremely considerate. Whatever others might say, you have been gracious although my colleagues and the public, including my family, talk ill of me. You know they speak out of jealousy and malign me, but you are All-knowing and no thought can be hidden from You. You are my friend in a friendless world.

'I have accepted only gifts and cash given out of goodwill by those whom I have served. Never demanded them. What one gives out of goodwill must be accepted with grace, say our Shastras, otherwise you will be hurting a good soul who wants to have the pleasure of giving.

'Apart from the *Ramayana*, I inherited from my father only common sense and the courage to face life under all circumstances. Through Your grace, I rose from the smallest job in the Revenue Department to the present position in the red building, occupying the tahsildar's seat.'

The tahsildar's office was the focal point where peasants arrived seeking various relief measures offered by the government and the government agencies. Mr Gurumurthi was the 'agency'. Peasants had to come to him for a variety of favours and present their applications for fertilizers, pesticides, spare parts for tractors, and for cash loans. All applications had to be rubber-stamped on his desk and initialled by him, and for each touch of his seal on any paper he had to be paid a certain sum of money, depending on the value of the request, discretely isolated from the quantum meant for the Treasury.

The isolated amount was propelled into the left-side drawer of his desk, only then did the applicant's paper become animated. When he closed the office for the day, Gurumurthi scooped out the contents of the drawer with loving fingers, and transferred them to a specially tailored inner pocket of his shirt, next to his skin where it gently heaved with his heartthrob. He enjoyed the feel of the wad nestling close to his heart.

He often reflected with satisfaction, 'No pick-pocket will have a chance. If everyone follows my method, pickpocketing will be eliminated, and those rogues will have to turn to honest jobs . . . perhaps to agriculture, and come to me for favours, who knows?' A questioning mind might ask at this point, 'Who is the real pickpocket?'

Always the last to leave, after making sure there was no embarrassing presence lurking in any corner of the office except the old attender at the door wearing a red sash across his shoulder, displaying a badge announcing, *Peon, Tahsildar's Office*, he was a discrete man who had watched a succession of tahsildars in his career.

Gurumurthi's wife, Saroja, used to be a quiet-going, peace-loving sort, even-tempered and minding her business. But with years, she began to play the role of the better-half, and became questioning, righteous, and argumentative. He noticed her transformation after the birth of their first daughter, Raji, who proved to be the best of the lot, the only one in the family who was at peace with herself and with the world.

She married a boy from a family who did not demand a dowry and were satisfied with a simple, inexpensive wedding. His wife, Saroja, suspected that the boy suffered from some deformity, and that his parents were anxious to marry him off anyhow. It was all an exaggeration, of course (Gurumurthi avoided a too close scrutiny). They turned out to be the happiest couple known, begetting three children in four years—twins at first and a single one later. They kept themselves to themselves, which was the best part of it.

Occasionally, Raji came down with her children; somewhat trying times those were, since her children were noisy and restless. Gurumurthi was not fond of grandchildren. Fortunately, the maximum time Raji could spare was one week, her husband needing her constant attention. Gurumurthi always felt relieved when she proposed to leave. Not so his wife, thoughtless woman, who would press her to stay on, until he put his foot down and said, 'Leave her alone; after all Raji knows her responsibilities.' He organized her departure with zest. He engaged a jutka to take her to the railway station, making sure that the girl had sufficient funds to pay the fare. At the ticket counter he held out his hand to her for money. He was in acute suspense till he bundled her and the children into a compartment within the five minutes' halt of the six o' clock Fast Express towards Trichy, and heaved a sigh of relief when the engine whistled and pulled out. He never permitted his wife to accompany them to the station explaining, 'I want to walk back, but if you come we may have to hire a jutka.'

'Not at all necessary. I can also walk home.'

'Don't be argumentative,' he sternly told her, and left her behind to watch Raji's departure from the doorstep. At the railway platform when the train moved he became emotional, ran along with it shouting, 'Raji, take good care of yourself and the children, and convey my blessings to your husband.'

His second daughter, Kamala, was married two years later. The family priest who generally carried a sheaf of horoscopes of eligible brides and grooms in his circuit was a busybody who, when not performing poojas, proposed marriage alliances among his clientele. One afternoon he sat down beside Gurumurthi's easy chair, and asked, 'Have you heard of Dr Cheema of Lawley Extension?'

'Of course who does not know him?' said Gurumurthi.

'His clinic is crowded all the time like a temple at festival time.'

'I know, I know,' said Gurumurthi, 'what about him?' It was a Sunday, and he relaxed all day in his easy chair. The priest sat cross-legged on the floor as became an orthodox Brahmin, who would not touch the leather covering on any seat (though it might be only rexine, resembling leather, who could be sure? He had two religious functions ahead and would have to take a bath if he touched leather and he avoided the risk of pollution by sitting cross-legged on the floor, which also pleased his patrons who were wealthy).

The priest continued, 'His son is twenty-one years old, and is studying for an auditor's job . . . . I don't know what degree he will get. Very bright boy, whenever I see him I think of our Kamala, such a perfect match. I always keep in hand our Kamala's horoscope, I compared it with that boy's, just out of curiosity. The horoscopes match perfectly—perfectly means, I do not know how to say it—like—like,' he quoted a Sanskrit verse from the Vedas which said, 'No power on earth or heaven could keep apart a couple whose stars are destined to merge.' He concluded, by asking, 'May I show them our Kamala's horoscope?'

The priest's instinct turned out to be sound, as there never was a happier couple in the world. Only the alliance proved acrimonious, and continued long after Kamala had left her parents' home and was happily settled in Lawley Extension with her husband. The doctor realized when the wedding ceremonies were over that Gurumurthi was unreliable. The doctor had agreed to a simple, unostentatious wedding, as suggested by Guru. 'Let us perform the ceremony at the hill temple, and hold a reception in Malgudi. I don't believe in wasting money just for a show and feeding a crowd. We could save that money and endow it as a fund for the young couple, so that they may have a good start in life.' The doctor appreciated the idea, since his son planned to go to America for higher studies and could utilize the fund thus saved. The priest was a go-between for the negotiations. Gurumurthi kept his wife and daughter out of earshot when discussing financial matters with the priest. He told them from time to time. 'Leave it to men to talk about these matters. Women should not interfere but mind their business.'

After the wedding the doctor kept reminding him of his promise to give Rs 50,000 saved from the wedding expenses. Gurumurthi prided himself secretly on managing to marry off both his daughters, without eroding his bank balance. Gurumurthi had simplified Kamala's marriage to such an extent that even Raji was not invited properly, and he spurned the idea whenever his wife reminded him to send them a formal announcement. 'All right, all right,' he said, brushing her off—'leave it to me. I know when to write.' And he reflected, 'Why should Raji be bothered to come with her crippled husband and the restless children, travelling all the way. Our outlook must change—a revolutionary change is needed in our society. Inviting a motley for every wedding is senseless, wonder who started this irrational practice.'

The doctor kept reminding him of the money due to his son, who was preparing to leave for America. Gurumurthi had perfected the art of dodging. He kept explaining that the delay was due to certain government bonds, which would mature soon. Gurumurthi had also promised the bridegroom two suits fit for American wear, for which he explained, he had ordered imported material from a firm in

Madras, and as soon as it was received the young man could straight go to his tailor and get himself measured out. He added, 'I know an excellent tailor who stitched suits for European planters settled in Mempi estates. His father also was a tailor to the British governors.' The proposal was gradually allowed to fade away. Next, for the Deepavali festival, Guru had promised a solitaire diamond ring for his son-in-law. After waiting for three months, the doctor himself arrived one afternoon to remind him. Guru received him with a lot of fuss, summoned his wife and daughter to come out and make an obeisance. Kamala was counting the days before she could get married. Her father was putting it off on the plea that they were passing through an inauspicious part of the year. But his real motive was to avoid the expenses of an orthodox nuptial ceremony. Guru felt that our whole civilization was rotten and involved wasteful expenditure at every turn. There was no one in whom he could confide his thoughts. His wife was too narrow-minded and conventional and would not understand his philosophy of life. Best policy would be to drift along without taking any decision; the inauspicious months giving him a sort of reprieve. The young couple met now and then and went out together; he was not so narrow-minded as to object to it—after all they were to be husband and wife. Once again it was his wife who displayed narrow prejudices—what would people say if a couple before the consummation ceremony met and roamed about? That was her upbringing, she was free to think as she liked, but he did not mind it, even hoped secretly that they would settle it between themselves and live happily ever after.

When the doctor on his present visit, after accepting all the snacks, broached the subject of the diamond ring, Guru hummed and hawed, 'Eh, ring, ring, of course,' he repeated reflectively. 'That goldsmith is very very slippery. What shall I do? Impossible man! Everyday I go there and shout at him. But what's the use? He promised and swore by all the gods and his ancestors that he would give the ring for Deepavali. But you see . . . .'

'Shall we both go and tackle him? He seems to be a crook . . . why not tell the police? I know the superintendent,' said the doctor. 'Yes, yes, of course, but only as a last resort . . . . He has been our jeweller for generations . . .'

The doctor got up and left. The lady of the house, who had been watching the scene from a corner came out like a fury, 'You are bringing shame on us. Is there no limit?'

'What limit?' Guru asked aggressively. 'He is avaricious, thinks diamond rings grow on trees . . . .'

At this point Kamala came out with eyes swollen with tears. 'Father, why did you promise it then?' she asked.

'Oh! Oh! You too! You should not be overhearing your elders talk.'

'I am not a baby,' she said. 'You should keep your promise, it is awkward for me. I can't face them if you dodge like this.'

'Oh, you have become their lawyer!' he said laughing cynically, 'I did not expect you to talk to me like this. You are more interested in those people—your father-in-law earns thousands everyday. Why can't he buy a diamond ring for his son, if he cares so much for him?'

'My husband does not care for diamonds or anything.'

'In that case why bother me? You will mind your business. Leave these matters to my judgement. Don't imitate your mother's manner. I'll see that you don't feel any embarrassment later. Be grateful I found you a husband—' Her mother said, 'It's no use talking to him,' turned round and tried to take her daughter away. But the girl stood firmly and persisted in saying, 'He doesn't care for a diamond or any ring, it's you that offered and promised.'

'Well, that's all old story, such promises are a formality between in-laws during Deepavali. One should not take such talks literally . . . .' Kamala could find no words to express her indignation, burst into tears, and withdrew. Her mother came out again like fury and shouted at Guru. He felt enraged and shouted back. 'It's impossible to live in this house! Everyone heckles me.' He briskly got up, put on his sandals, and walked out. He reached the corner of Vinayak Street, where he saw Rao the stamp-vendor standing at his door. 'These are bad days—' said Guru. The other readily agreed with him and added, 'What with the prices going up, do you notice the price of brinjals? Impossible to buy vegetables, and such extravagant public expenditure by the government everywhere without any consideration for the public.'

'Even in private life so much extravagance we see, our women are old-fashioned and still continue old practices and ceremonials and presents, with Deepavali growing into a sort of trade, what with crackers, and fireworks, silks and diamonds! Such a waste! The only solution is education. Our women must be educated,' said Guru.

'When they get educated they become arrogant,' said the other man. 'Do you know how my brother's wife talks to him, because she is a graduate?'

'We are passing through hopeless days, on the whole. Even without a BA degree my wife insists on this and that and must have her own way in everything. It is bound to get worse, if we don't do something about it.'

'True, true,' said the other one, feeling satisfied that he had agreed with a tahsildar, and did not contradict him in any manner. A tahsildar exercised his authority in several directions, and it was safer to be on agreeable terms with him. His seal on an application was indispensable especially to a 'stamp-vendor' whose livelihood depended on vending all denominations of special paper for legal documents.

When Guru reached home he found the street door ajar with no one in sight. He stood at the doorway and shouted, 'What is the matter? Where is everybody hiding and why?' His wife screamed back from an unseen corner, 'Why have you got into the habit of shouting? No one is playing hide-and-seek here.'

'Oh, you aren't? I am glad to hear that. Where is Kamala?'

'She was writing a letter, must have gone out to post it.'

'Letters, oh, letters! To whom?'

'She doesn't have to declare it to anyone.'

'Oh, is that so, mistake to have sent her to college. Women become educated and arrogant.'

His wife shouted back from her room, 'What has come over you today?'

'That's what I want to ask you all? I made a mistake in staying away from office today. You people don't seem to appreciate my company at home . . . . I will go back to my work . . . .'

'Yes, do so. It's profitless to be away from your office table, I suppose!' she said emerging from her room.

'But for my drudgery, you would not live in a house like this, or have those bangles and necklace . . .'

'Why this kind of talk?'

'Something has gone wrong, you have lost all sense of humour, take everything literally and seriously like our Kamala's doctor father-in-law. I only wanted to remind you that you came with a battered tin trunk . . . as a new bride, even the railway porter did not demand more than four annas to carry it on his head.'

'And what did you bargain him down to actually?'

she asked. He laughed and said, 'You have still got your sense of humour—I was wrong in saying that you had lost it. The trunk did not weigh much, I am sure, otherwise the porter would have demanded one rupee.'

'The box had in it forty sovereigns only, which my father gave me, these bangles and chain also . . . they don't weigh much inside a trunk. After that there was no addition in my box or on my person.'

'What happened to the sovereigns?'

'Don't you remember that the two daughters had to be married off but they could not be presented bare-necked and without bangles on their wrists at their weddings, and had to be provided with a minimum of jewellery.'

'Why didn't you tell me?'

She spurned to answer his question and left his company. He kept looking in her direction and reflected. 'Impossible to carry on any useful talk with women, always ready to squander and argue about it. Forty sovereigns to be squandered on tinsel to impress in-laws! But after all, her father chose to give her a mere pittance but did not have the courtesy to tell me! What do I care what that battered tin box contained, so long ago? That box itself, where is it? Lost with all the junk when we moved here.'

It was a provocative subject, revived whenever the lady wanted to score a point. 'You have managed to bring along all your old things, particularly that unsightly, uncomfortable sofa in which no one could sit in peace.'

'I did not bring it in, knowing what you would say.'

'Not a word could I ever say about your treasures, although I wanted to keep my trunk and repair it . . . that would have made it new . . . .'

'It was too battered, broken, rusty, discoloured in patches, had only a single handle on one side, the other came off when the porter touched it—no wonder your father chose to put his forty sovereigns in it. He knew no one would be tempted to touch that tin trunk.'

'Not worse than the sofa, your heirloom which you chose to bring all the way though it'd have saved money to break its legs and use them for heating water for a bath.'

'I brought it along with other goods in that bullock-cart, didn't have to pay extra money for it. With a little polish and a pat here and there, it will fetch at least two hundred rupees.'

'Then why don't you sell it?'

'How does it bother you? After all I have dumped it in the cow-shed—'

'Cow-shed! When are we buying the cow for the shed? If it comes, the sofa will be in the next lane I suppose, for any vagrant looking for trash or firewood.'

'Aren't you terrified of the milk price today?' he asked, changing the subject.

'No need to worry about it, as you have successfully abolished coffee at home,' she said.

'The smell of coffee is nauseating,' he said.

'But I love coffee, and find it hard to do without it.'

'No use thinking of it, you must have got used to being without it by now. It is not indispensable. I have brought up our daughters without coffee, they never had a craving for it. Two meals with good rice and vegetables will be sufficient to make one a giant.'

'Our daughters have left this house because they didn't want to grow into giants under your care . . . .'

'How do you say daughters? Only Raji is gone, and in Trichy.'

'Have you not noticed that Kamala who went out to post a letter has not returned, even after three hours? She won't come back. I promise it. She does not want to talk to you again.'

'It's a conspiracy,' he looked angry and upset. 'When will she come back? Where is she?'

'She packed up her clothes and left for Lawley Extension in a jutka—'

'I should not have left you both alone to hatch this plot.'

'Don't call it a plot, she has only joined her husband. Thank God he loves her and could persuade his father not to bother about the gifts you promised.'

'What about the formal nuptial ceremony?'

'They will manage it without public fuss, between themselves.'

Guru let out a hearty laugh. 'Very clever, without a paisa expense—'

'Do you know my father spent Rs 10,000 for our nuptials at our village, inviting a hundred guests for a three-day nuptial celebration—you welcomed it then.'

'I was young and let my elders decide things—'

'Also because the money they squandered was not yours.'

He was in his seat transacting business as usual, with a crowd of villagers waiting for his favours. His badge-wearing door-keeper who usually stood outside came in excitedly and whispered, 'Collector is coming.' Before he could complete his sentence the collector, the chief officer of the district, walked in, and Gurumurthi rose to his feet deferentially. The peon tried to disperse the crowd of applicants, but the collector said, 'Leave them alone.' He said, 'Sit down,' to the tahsildar, who, however, kept standing since the collector himself did not sit but moved around inspecting the office, its furniture, and the load of files in a shelf behind the tahsildar. He asked, 'Those are applications in front of you?'

'Yes, sir.'

'Give me those papers.' With trepidation the tahsildar handed over the papers. The collector flicked through them still standing. 'Please take your seat, sir,' Gurumurthi said offering his seat. The collector occupied the seat, spread out the papers on the tables, and scrutinized them. 'Why have you kept them pending so long?'

'Some details are awaited—some of the applications are incomplete.'

The collector picked up a couple of applications, studied them and asked, 'Who are these applicants?'

Before the tahsildar could find an answer, two men from the group came forward, 'They are our applications, your honour.'

'When did you present them at this office?'

'Four months ago, sir . . . .'

'Why have you not sanctioned those loans yet?'

'They are not able to produce their birth certificates, sir.'

The collector asked them, 'Why have you failed to produce the certificates?'

'Our village *karnam* is dead and the new man—'

The collector turned to Gurumurthi and said, 'Very unsatisfactory. You could have taken their sworn statement and attested them.'

'We have been coming here, your honour, every day—walking from our village, leaving our work—'

The collector summoned Gurumurthi to his office next day and said, 'You may go on leave from tomorrow.'

'May I know the reason, sir?'

'Not one reason, but several, I get reports and know what's going on—'

'Oh, sir, there are gossip-mongers and tale-bearers all around.'

'Farmers come all the way to seek help and relief promised to them, and you delay and play with them some game.'

'I am doing my best, sir, but they won't follow the procedure.'

'I know what you are trying to say—excuses you are inventing. Don't want all that—I know what's going on in your office. You are a senior official—I don't want to be too hard on you. I could take disciplinary steps, but I'm giving you the choice of taking all the leave at your credit, and seek voluntary retirement at the end of it. If you don't want this choice, I'll have to recommend to the government an inquiry and further steps.'

The man was shaken at first, but survival seemed more important, he remembered a saying: 'If the head is threatened let the headgear be blown off.' An inquiry would ruin him; they could withhold his pension and confiscate his property. Gurumurthi acted also as a moneylender, on the side, to the villagers approaching him for interest-free loans offered by the government, by his delaying tactics.

He got over the initial shock in course of time and adjusted himself to a retired life. He assured his wife, 'We have enough to live on. Our daughters are married, and we have this house, the rents from those shops and my pension. What do I care? That young man, the collector, seems to be an upstart, I don't care. Everyone says he has been doing this sort of mischief in every district. He demanded certain explanations, but I firmly told him that I don't care to explain and am prepared to go. I demanded all the leave at my credit and then retirement. I told him that I have drudged for this ungrateful government long enough—'

'What caste is he?' Saroja asked.

'I don't know. Whatever it may be, he is an upstart and is out to eliminate all the seniors in the service.

When he found I was tough, he came down a step or two and tried to coax and cajole me to stay, but I was firm, made him understand that they do not deserve a conscientious hard-working man but only a hollow, showy scoundrel—who would cringe for their favours.'

'But it was rumoured that you were not helpful to the villagers and so the collector—' He cut her short, 'Nonsense, don't listen to gossip-mongers . . . . You would not be living in this style if I didn't work hard. After all your father was only a schoolmaster.'

'And yet you demanded a dowry from him!'

'Why do you bother about it now, so long ago! If he hadn't found the resources for a modest dowry, he'd have got a bankrupt son-in-law, not one who could support a family.'

He organized his retired life satisfactorily. He left home every morning, went out and spent his time in the free reading room at the corner, a little den with newspapers old and new, piled on a small table at the centre, and a shelf full of odd volumes discarded in the neighbourhood. Some evenings he went and sat on a bench at the Jubilee Park, where gathered pensioners like him, and Rao, the stamp-vendor, would of course be there. They discussed the state of the nation and the problems of each other's health. From time to time he visited his banker on Market Road to watch the savings burgeoning with monthly interests. Such moments away from home seemed to him beneficial as he could avoid his argumentative wife. Morning hours were her worst time according to him as she seemed too tense. After lunch she mellowed, and at about seven o'clock in the evening she visited the temple. When she was away, he relaxed in his canvas chair and got absorbed in some odd volume picked up at the free reading room. After dinner was a tranquil and peaceful time unless she opened her gambit with, 'I met so and so in the temple, do you know what she remarked?'

'You women seem to have no better business than gossiping—' it would start thus and then go on until both got tired and sleepy.

Time passed. One day Gurumurthi brought out a proposition, which sounded light at first but proved portentous. He had hesitated till he found her in a receptive mood and then brought out the proposition.

'Saroja, we must have a son—' She was taken aback.

'What! At our age?' she exclaimed and was amused. He explained, 'Not that way. We can adopt.' She still treated it as a joke. Sitting on the pyol after dinner and enjoying the night breeze and listening to the rustle of leaves of the rain-tree, they were in a pleasant mood. She asked, 'Adopt? How? What do you mean.' He elaborated, 'We are old, our daughters live their own lives away from us—'

'Why not?'

He fumbled on, 'We are aged. . . .'

'Nothing surprising. No one grows younger in this

world—' At this point she heard the rattle of vessels in the kitchen and dashed away muttering. 'It's that cat again—'

'I don't know how to talk to her—she either laughs or gets angry and argues.' He had to wait for a propitious time. Next day he was determined to get it out of his system. He called suddenly, 'Saroja, come here. I am serious about it—' She was cleaning a corner of the hall with a broom and mop. He was sitting, as usual, in his canvas chair beside the window.

'I want to explain something.' She dropped her broom and stood beside him. 'Now listen—as we grow old, we need a son to look after us.'

'Why this sudden decision? Are you serious?'

'I've told you I am serious. I can do many things without waiting for your opinion but now—'

'Yes, that's how I have lived—even our daughters' marriages, you never waited for my opinion—you were the one who made all the decisions. Women must not listen when you talk to the priest about financial matters. You are convinced that I don't know how to count cash over two rupees—I don't even know if you are rich or poor.' Gurumurthi realized that he had started her off on a dangerous track inadvertently. 'You are the Supreme Lord and I am only a dependant not worth talking to,' she concluded. He realized that he had no chance to broach the subject, which was obsessing his mind. Though normally he was the master of any situation, today he felt somewhat puzzled, yet decided to bully her to listen to him, the only way to get along in family affairs as he had known all his life. He said firmly, 'I want to adopt a son, and that is all to it.' She took a little time to understand the implications, stood silently awhile and asked, 'What do you expect me to say?'

'Show some interest—that's all—'

She turned round and went back to her corner. He felt infuriated, got up, followed her, caught her by the shoulder, turned her round to face him, looked into her eyes, and repeated firmly: 'You must hear me fully.' Tears flowed down her cheeks as she shook herself free. 'Do what you like why should you bother me?'

'Adoption means by both parents—you have a part in the ceremony. Otherwise I do not have to ask you. You don't even ask who is the son?'

'I have said do what you please.'

'Should you not know who is going to be the son? I'll tell you though, since it's my duty, even if you are indifferent—my brother Sambu's third son. He is ready to give him to us—'

She said, 'You mean Ragu! He is a monkey—I won't live in this house, if you bring him here—'

Gurumurthi shouted, 'You are challenging me?' and went back to his chair fretting. 'She thinks she can order me about because I am gentle and considerate. I won't allow this sort of thing anymore and must put her in her place. I have refrained from mentioning why a son is needed—to save her feelings, but I'll tell her even if it upsets her, I don't care—' He got up resolutely, went up to her and shouted, 'You know why? When I die, I want a son to light the funeral pyre and perform the rites, otherwise . . . .'

'Otherwise what?' she asked. He glared at her speechlessly. She continued, 'Life or death is not anyone's choice, we can't know.' He laughed ironically, 'Oh, you are becoming a philosopher too, hm! You are listening too much to discourses in the evenings. Hereafter you had better stay away from those discourses at the temple . . . . '

'You had better stay away from the stamp-vendor at the corner house. Ever since you retired from service you have nothing better to do than listen to his advice and gossip at the reading room.'

'Why do you talk ill of him! Shut up and don't talk of people you do not know . . . .'

Now that she had got over the initial shock, she got into a taunting mood, and added, 'Did that stamp-vendor not mention also that if a son is not available your grandchildren can perform the rites? Anyway why do you cultivate these unhappy thoughts.'

He pursued his plan methodically. He called his family priest and consulted him in whispers, while his wife ignored them and all their activity and minded her business. Gurumurthi wrote to his brother in Dindigul a closely-written postcard every day and awaited the arrival of the postman morning and evening, and kept talking about the arrangements as the date approached. What made him uneasy was that he was expected to buy new clothes for his brother and his wife and for himself and his wife too. He felt he could save on this item, as he preserved the clothes presented to him and Saroja at festivals or other occasions by village applicants seeking his goodwill. Saroja only warned him, 'They have been in storage for years and may have a musty smell.' He said, 'Don't create problems, please put them out for airing, I'll get some napthalene balls also . . . I don't mind the expense.'

'You get a dozen for half a rupee—' she said puckishly.

'You seem to know everything ,' he remarked.

The priest had explained, 'Adoption is a very sacred matter, holier than all other activities. You must realize the sanctity of it. All gods and planetary deities must be satisfied with offerings in a homa through Agni, the God of Fire. You will be acquiring a new entity, body and soul, and will assume the responsibilities for his welfare. Your brother has five sons and it will be no loss to him to give one away; at the same time you will gain merit by adopting a son. He must solemnly vow before the fire that he will be your dutiful son all his life and perform all the necessary rites when you join your revered ancestors.' Gurumurthi had also heard on the park-bench a general statement from a member, 'When you bring up a minor son in your custody, you can also demand a rebate on your tax.'

With the arrival of Ragu, a lanky youth of twelve, Saroja made her exit, having remained monosyllabic and silent all through. She had performed her duties mechanically, just obeying the directions of the priest, who had told her to sit beside her husband, join him in offering oblations in the holy fire. She prostrated at her husband's feet when directed, clasped his hand, received Ragu with open arms formally when told to, seated him on her lap and fed him with a piece of banana, sugar, honey and milk, sniffed his forehead, and touched it with sandal paste.

The smoke from the holy fire permeated every corner of the house, the smell of burnt faggots lingered in the air irritating their eyes, long after the ceremony, which ended at mid-day. The priest and four Brahmins departed at three in the afternoon; after they left, Gurumurthi rested in his easy chair and fell asleep. Ragu sat on the pyol and watched the street. He would have loved to go out and wander about but his 'father' had warned him not to go out alone, and so he sat there moping. His own parents had left soon after the ceremony. When everybody was gone, Saroja came out of her room carrying a small jute bag and roll of bedding. A jutka stood at the door. She stepped out softly, after hesitating for a minute in front of her husband, unable to decide whether to wake him or not. She felt it'd be unnecessary to take leave of him. She had already told him she was leaving after the adoption ceremony, explaining that she was going back to her village in Karur in order to take care of her old mother who was lonely and helpless after her husband's death two years before.

Ragu lived as the son of the house for four days, greatly puzzled by his new life. He had never thought he would have to live permanently in the company of his uncle, who insisted upon being addressed as 'father'. The boy felt uneasy in his grim company, and found it difficult to laugh at his jokes, or listen to his observations, suggestions, obvious advices and moralizing, and above all his awkward storytelling. Gurumurthi depended on Pankaja Vilas for his sustenance, but the boy did not find that food adequate or acceptable. His 'father' watching him all the time, he was never allowed to go out except in his company to sit on the park-bench and listen to his cronies. The boy stood it for four days, secretly longing for his companions playing cricket in Dindigul streets, and one afternoon slipped away while his 'father' was asleep.

Gurumurthi searched for the boy here and there and spent sleepless nights until a postcard arrived from Dindigul to say that the boy was back there and would join him after obtaining his school-leaving certificate. Obviously it was never obtained. The boy kept away, nor did his father write to Gurumurthi again, Gurumurthi wrote once or twice, never got a reply, and decided not to waste money on postage anymore. He reflected, 'After all it is all for the best, why should I keep that boy? And what for? Difficult to understand him. It has cost me less than seven hundred rupees and a 150 in rail fare for the parents to come for the ceremony and fifty rupees for feeding the priests; after all it made only a slight dent in my bank balance, that's all; and my brother's demand for a 'loan' of five thousand rupees, which I promised to consider though fully aware that it was a veiled price tag on the boy, need not be given now, that would have been another extravagance if that boy had stayed on. Also the boy was too demanding, always wanting something to eat, frowning at Pankaja Vilas food, he was a glutton, could not be satisfied with a simple nutritious meal. It was also a strain to keep him amused or entertained, the fellow sticking to him, all the time—Raji and Kamala as children were never like this fellow, they left him alone unless called to his side. Good riddance on the whole.' He felt complacent, except when he was told by the stamp-vendor, 'The boy is only twelve, but when he attains majority, he may legally demand a partition and a share of your property especially if he should come over and perform the funeral rites when you die.' Gurumurthi felt uneasy at this prospect but comforted his mind with the proviso: 'Only if he performs my funeral ceremony, but why should I tell him or anyone of my death?'

III

TABLE TALK

TABLE TALK

I BEGIN TO DOUBT MY WISDOM IN BUYING A TV set investing ten thousand rupees for the luxury. Now I want my money back, if the Ministry will take it and give me bonds, even if they are non-convertible, until my great-grandson celebrates his thousandth moon. Here, in Mysore we receive only the National Programme which means mostly Hindi programmes for five hours at a stretch, while one sits through hoping that at least the next item may make sense. Profound and prolonged interviews, features and reports, not to speak of entertainment, are fed to us in massive doses but in a language which though pleasant to the ear, conveys no meaning. After prolonged exposure extending over months, I have come to understand only two words—*samachar* and *samapt.* To be shut up in a little room with a loudspeaker blaring, used to be an ingenious form of political torture in certain European countries at one time, now to be compelled to sit through a prolonged session listening to an unintelligible language seems also a torment, though in a lesser degree. Someone seems to have hit upon it as a brilliant strategy: 'Anti-Hindiwallas won't accept Hindi? Is it? All right. We will deal with them. Force-feed them. Subject them to a barrage, and they will inevitably come round. How do circus animals begin to understand and perform? Only through repeated auditory attack. How can anyone not understand Hindi? Sheer cursedness—opposed to National integration. Anti-Hindiwallas hope to hang onto English by pretending not to understand Hindi, that's all. Down with English.' As a result of this philosophy, we have to sit before our TV every evening through the *Krishi* programme, various serials, and another and another, with forbearance, without understanding a word, sometimes wildly guessing the meaning. Even thus, some of the programmes have become our favourites. We have grown used to certain personalities appearing on the TV screen, and watch and try to extract some sense from their gestures and antics and the noise they make. Each one on this side of the TV screen in the family circle interprets the goings-on in his or her own way. The most respected linguist in our midst is the lady of the house who, years ago, studied Hindi and attained *visharad rashtra* status. She was preparing to scale further heights of *bhasha* until the Government of India came down with a declaration of language policy, which caused public disorder and the lady gave up her academic pursuit promptly. Now she has forgotten whatever she had learnt, but remains our sole interpreter in the TV room. One of us may ask, 'Who is this new character?'

She will say, 'O! That is the smuggler's cousin.' 'No, he seems to be the second son of the *Humlog* family. How did you get the idea that he was a smuggler?' Another may say, 'That man in the embroidered *kurta* looks like a smuggler.'

'Somehow you seem to conclude that anyone wearing an embroidered shirt is a smuggler.' Or the next question may be: 'What is that girl saying, when her elders are discussing her marriage?'

'Actually that girl is the wife of the smart doctor and they were all discussing their holiday plans.'

'But the doctor is a bachelor—'

'He is not. Did you not notice the girl at his side on the sofa?'

'She was only a patient waiting to show her tongue.'

Thus go on our speculations, until a welcome advice is heard: 'Next programme will be the news in Hindi. Let us switch off and go in for our supper.' And so we avoid the news in Hindi since we will be seeing the same VIPs and Conferences in the English news also. We avoid Hindi news not only because of its obscurity but also the deadly monotony of delivery. However, when the English news comes, we realize that we are no better off. Once again monotony from grim newsreaders who look desperate and in a hurry to reach the last line of the script within the allotted time, and grin with unconcealed relief, only when they say, 'Good-night'. However, young ladies who announce the coming programmes carry it off, though they lisp and sigh and whisper and drop sibilants rather than words. No one minds anything they do because they are invariably charming which dissolves it all.

I will end this with a few constructive hints:

- Let us have English subtitles and summaries of stories. That way Hindi will be gradually understood and in the years to come you may find us on par with, say, our fellow citizens in Madhya Pradesh.

- As a gesture of reciprocal courtesy, north Indian stations should telecast national programmes also in Tamil, Telugu, Malayalam, Kannada (by turns, of course) five hours each day, three days in a week. Thereby we shall achieve national integration.

- Fanatical avoidance of English is unnecessary and absurd, also against the spirit of Jawaharlal Nehru's promise to us. In a *Janavani* programme recently, should not the lady, (who I presume was a Minister of Health from the eminent seat she occupied) have had the goodness to give intelligible advice to a Madrassi who narrated a long tale of woe of his experience in a hospital. He had had an accident and had to go through a major operation at the hospital, and later had to go through a series of further operations, owing to some mistakes in the handling of his case at the first stage, and then he had to undergo prolonged treatment for a variety of infections acquired at the hospital ward from linen, food and surroundings. The Minister appeared to give him a patient hearing, but vouched no direct reply. She suddenly turned to the officer and spoke volubly in impeccable Hindi, leaving the complainant, as well as us, guessing. She might, probably have ordered the immediate liquidation of the poisonous hospital. Or she might have said, 'Let the wretch learn Hindi before presuming to criticize our medical services. Meanwhile keep the file pending until the man approaches us again properly.'

LOOKING FOR MAGSAYSAY

One

TEODORO R. YANGCO, WHO OWNED THE Try-Tran Transport Company, needed a mechanic, and Magsaysay, still a student then, presented himself for the job. Yangco instinctively approved of the lad who had come in search of part-time employment. The young man was given a start of thirty pesos a month, after a couple of weeks of trial.

Within a short period, Yangco felt gratified with his choice. Here was this young man with heart and ears attuned to the sound of an internal combustion engine. He would examine the shade of the smoke emitted at the exhaust, listen intently while the engine idled and watch a bus as it started off, and his examination did not stop with the workshop. On his way to the college, if he saw a Try-Tran bus on the road, he watched its performance, made a mental note if something seemed to him wrong, and tackled it at the first opportunity.

Yangco doubled his salary within a very short time. He appreciated the fact that Magsaysay could not only explain academically what was wrong with a vehicle, he could also roll up his sleeves and crawl under it, if necessary. He found that within the first few months of the young man's arrival his repair and replacement bills were going down. He gave him a further rise and soon Magsaysay was drawing eighty pesos a month.

Quite a rich man now, but it was not in his nature to grab and hold money. His needs were simple—he never drank and he had no interest either in foppishness or in luxury. No wonder then that eighty pesos seemed to him a big sum, and he dealt out his money to all and sundry. Throughout his life he felt a slight inadequacy of money that all liberal temperaments experience. He was always hospitable to old friends or relatives who came to Manila and needed help. He had a very sturdy philosophy about money; not to bother oneself too much about it.

Yangco's allowance saw him through his course at José Rizal College and, by the time he finished his studies he was promoted to shop superintendent in the organization. He was the most energetic member of the company. He was here, there and everywhere. He never regarded any branch of work as not his and never waited to be told what to do. He worked at his desk, supervised the workshop activities, went out to check the collections on the road, came back, went out again to look for a spare part noticed earlier in a junk heap. He had the thrill of a hunter when he set out on such missions. No one in the company enjoyed doing his job as much.

*

Yangco's company was destined to play a large part in his personal life. Magsaysay's was a basically simple, disciplined life; he was always busy and did not have much time to brood over the other sex or to take much notice of women. He remained in this state of ascetic indifference until he met Luz, his future wife.

If ever there was an example of love at first sight, here was one. Luz Benzon came of an aristocratic family in Balanga. Father Benzon had sold a transport company to Yangco and had sent up Luz and her sister to collect the money from the latter. Luz was a high school girl, sixteen years old, and extremely attractive. When she and her sister were conferring with the manager, Magsaysay entered the office, presumably on some business, but stood arrested at the sight of the girls. (It was Luz who had attracted his attention.) There are rumours that this was not the first time that he saw her and that he had given the sisters a lift in his car on an earlier occasion.

He probably forgot to explain why he had come to the manager's office, and went back to his workshop in a thoughtful mood. He surveyed himself critically; he was in an oil-stained overall, a perfect uniform for getting into the repair pit, but hardly the right thing for the present moment. Nothing could be done about it now. He realized that time was running short and that unless he acted he might lose sight of the girl once for all.

His mind never worked at greater speed. It was not in his nature to waver and he arrived at a quick, practical decision. He must know where she lived, and then he could start investigating who she was. Already, he was beginning to feel that it would be impossible for him to exist without doing something about her. He saw a car outside with a chauffeur and boldly going up to him, asked him to go away. He put on a casual tone and said: 'The ladies have some more work; you may take the car and go; we will send them in one of ours when they are ready.'

When the two girls emerged from the building, Magsaysay had his car drawn up ready. His throat must have gone dry when he saw his vision coming down the steps. He had never thought that his scheme would work so well. He cleared his throat and mumbled an explanation, struggling not to be caught staring at Luz.

'Why?' asked one of the girls and, since he could

not give a normal answer, he just held the door of the car open, muttering: 'I can drive you anywhere you like.'

They got in without paying much attention to who was driving. He started the car and, when it moved, nearly gasped at his own duplicity and the success of his stratagem. He drove them through a circuitous route to their hostel. They were absorbed in their own talk and hardly noticed where they were going, only Luz noted that, now and then, while he drove, instead of keeping his eyes on the road, he was looking at the rear-view mirror.

Sunday was visitors' day at the girls' hostel. Luz received a message in her dormitory that her brother was waiting downstairs. Wondering whether it might be Aurelio or Augustin, she put away her books and went down to the reception hall. She looked about, did not see either brother, but only the tall mechanic from Yangco. He had tidied himself up, brushed back his hair and wore a tie and coat.

Without wasting time, he went up to her, holding a bouquet of roses in his hand. 'I have brought this for you,' he said, shyly. She understood. No words of explanation were called for or were available. She received the bouquet with a dry, soft 'Thanks', lingered for a while, turned and went back to her dormitory.

On all the subsequent visitors' days, this 'brother' turned up at the reception hall, always bearing some token—a flower, a sweet, a small gift. He went through his task at Yangco with his usual thoroughness and sense of duty, but his thoughts were elsewhere. It was not only an honourable courtship, but a persistent one. Filipino custom is not unlike Indian. Parental sanction, even as a matter of form, must be secured before a couple can become engaged. Magsaysay was fortunate to earn the goodwill of Luz's father also.

When the schools closed for summer, Luz returned to her home in Balanga. Love, as Magsaysay had already demonstrated, laughs at locksmiths, receptionists and the gate-keepers of a convent; now he was to prove that it could neutralize kilometres too. Balanga was one hundred miles from Manila and Magsaysay motored this distance every evening.

Luckily for him he was in a business where there was no shortage of conveyance. He would snatch a supper and start off. At the Balanga house, he was quite pleased to be left to stand away and watch Luz, speak to her when a chance came, never forcing himself on her attention. He started on his return journey only when they were ready to put out the lights in the house. It meant going to bed late several nights a week. He had to drive back one hundred miles, over a road that was none too good, snatch a few hours' sleep and go to the office early in the morning.

Luz's was an aristocratic household with many visitors at all times. Often there was some party or the other, and young men of wealth and social position came as suitors. Sometimes the sight of them filled Magsaysay with dismay. Their chances of winning the hand of Luz seemed far greater; but he never underrated himself. He was confident—the same assurance and confidence that he displayed later in his life (in politics and war) sustained him now.

He knew that, though Luz was not demonstrative, he could depend on her. Moreover, her father, contrary to the pattern in such matters, was really impressed with him. He liked the young man for his restraint, his helpfulness (often Magsaysay set right his automobile and drove him to Manila for a baseball match), and instinct told him that here was a young man who would go far. And he had made up his mind secretly not to oppose his proposal. He watched how Luz reacted to his presence. It is said that Magsaysay had to be patient for two years, and that he wore out three automobiles of Yangco Corporation. Luz and he were formally married on 30 June 1933, at the Lourdes Church, in Intramuros.

*

On 7 December 1941, Japan attacked Pearl Harbour and destroyed a great part of the American Navy and Air Force stationed there. Apart from the other consequences, well known to history, the effect on the course of Magsaysay's life was profound. His quiet existence, hitherto circumscribed by his domestic life in San Antonio and the arrival and departure of the Try-Tran buses, was over. He was uprooted from his well-defined routine and was catapulted into the world at large. After Pearl Harbour, the Japanese turned their attention to the Philippines. The entire Pacific area was in the process of being churned up and the Japanese Navy attacked and destroyed the American air base at Iba, capital of Zambales, and then the Clark Airfield.

In the Philippines, there had been all along an uneasy period of expectation, and now it was on them. Every Filipino realized that he should do his best to support America, and those who had already been in the reserve category offered to join up now. Magsaysay had no doubt received military training before, but he was not in the reserve category. He could only apply as a volunteer as thousands of other civilians had done.

Try-Tran played an important part in this area, offering transport facilities for the evacuation of the forces. The West Central Command covered the province of Zambales under Captain MacGuire. Magsaysay happened to know the captain and on 5 April 1942, he became a guerilla officer, together with a number of other volunteers. Colonel Thorpe who had been in charge of the guerillas in the whole of the Luzon area with his headquarters in Mount Pinatubo, after the fall of Bataan and Corregidor, was captured and executed by the Japanese. The various units that had been formed by him had to carry on their activities by themselves, according to their own judgement. The guerilla strategy had undergone a change now. The Japanese were ruthlessly dragging their nets about to catch the guerilla units and destroy them. And it became necessary to reduce their size in order to be out of view, and to avoid detection and destruction.

The guerilla fighters re-grouped themselves, went into hiding, with the Filipino members operating in Manila. These latter were to move about like ordinary civilian citizens, but were actually to act as a link between the hidden forces and the outside world. The units, scattered in the mountain regions of Zambales, were practically cut off from the outside world. They had to be provided with supplies as well as with information and their directives had to be carried out. They had to work out a wide scheme to destroy the Japanese forces.

To call Magsaysay a cog in this vast concealed machinery would be a mistake and hardly just to one who had thrown himself so heartily into the fray. He had a temperament that did not permit him to do anything except with his whole being, whether managing Try-Tran, repairing a vehicle, building a house or wooing his bride—he put himself intensely into it without reserve or hesitation.

His activities now were underground. He had let out his own house to a tenant and had rented a house in an obscure part of Manila. (He changed his residence a number of times within the next few years, all through the period of Japanese occupation.) He performed a variety of hazardous duties as an underground soldier. Not only did he operate a secret radio to give and take instructions, he gathered supplies and sent them up, under the very nose of the watchful Japanese, to Captain MacGuire's units.

He had also to collect arms and distribute them, in addition to looking after his own family. Medicine, food, arms, ammunition and information—everything had to move through an organized underground channel. He had his own elaborate network behind the placid, eventless face of Manila city and from here it reached out to the Zambales headquarters. Everything had to move smoothly, speedily. Any hitch or delay might mean starvation for his associates or even annihilation. It was not a programme that lasted merely for a week or a month but continued relentlessly over a period of two years—one year in the mountains hunting the Japanese and in turn being hunted by them, and another in Manila itself.

There was a price on Magsaysay's head—a hundred thousand pesos (US $ 50,000). It was reported that the Japanese raided his house in Manila and left after questioning him. His name was known but not his person. No one could easily mark him out. The constant danger which overhung one's head like a storm-cloud, the sturdy will to survive, the selfless acts, the arduous hide-and-seek with a price on one's head, all those moments of comparative lull during which one pretended to be living a normal life, and the terror in store if found out . . . . Romanticization, self-dramatization—these occur in retrospect. But the actor himself would hardly have been aware of the intensely dramatic nature of his existence in those two years of Japanese occupation and the two-and-a-half uncertain years of Collaborator rule.

Colonel Merril, who soon took all the guerilla organizations in Zambales under his control, nominated Magsaysay as a district commander. On the secret advice from General MacArthur's headquarters, Magsaysay had to get his area ready for the landing of American troops. It meant evacuation of a large number of people.

The residents were advised orally by the District Command to leave for the interior. All instructions had to be carried out without rousing the suspicion of the Japanese. Streams of people moved inland carrying their belongings. The plan was to co-ordinate the landing of the forces with an all-out attack on the enemy installations and airfields. The commander had a difficult task to perform.

As the evacuation began, groups of people stopped at Magsaysay's headquarters to plead with him to put off the attack as they feared reprisals in the event of the plan failing. He felt moved by their appeal and realized how the people had been reduced to a state of nervousness—valuing only their survival from day to day—by the four years of enemy rule. He said to them: 'We have to do this. The area between Olangapo and San Felipe has to be cleared and we cannot help it in any way. I calculate that our attack on the Japanese will end their terror here, but if we fail and you are to suffer for it, let me suffer first with you. I shall not wait for the Japanese; I shall ask you to take me and my family to the churchyard at Castillejos and put us before a firing-squad.'

*

Midnight of 16 January 1945, was fixed as the

moment for attack. Magsaysay had planned every detail carefully. He had chosen his men and deployed them skilfully. At midnight, flares on the mountain-tops of Malaplap gave the signal to those far away waiting to pounce upon the Japanese strip between Castillejos and Marcellino. The mountain overlooked the two towns and the air-strip was located between them. Commandos fell on sentries; squads fired on the barracks; a group of men crawled towards the planes and set them on fire with bottles of gasoline. Hangars and ammunition dumps shared the same fate. The enemy radio station at San Antonio was also destroyed simultaneously so that the adjoining Japanese garrisons were not aware of the fate of their compatriots in this part of the country.

The strategy now was to deal with the Japanese pockets individually; it was a prolonged and painstaking task but this was the only way it could be dealt with since the enemy had spread out everywhere into the mountains, the barrios, the fields and the forests in tentacle fashion. And although the main body had now been gradually withdrawn, the tentacles were still quite effective in dealing with the local population and keeping them under surveillance.

Guerilla tactics were the only effective method that could be adopted against such a powerful enemy. The guerillas were equipped with the latest types of arms now, having had an air-drop from time to time; still all of them were not armed with orthodox battle weapons, some had to do with bamboos, stones or whatever they could get hold of. With all this assorted armament, they gave such a thorough routing to the occupying forces, at least in this part of the country, that the American forces landed a fortnight later without firing a shot.

Two

On 31 August 1950, which happened to be Magsaysay's birthday, Speaker Perez, who had always supported him in all his plans and whose faith in him was immense, spoke to President Quirino about the desirability of making Magsaysay the Defence Secretary. His recommendation bore immediate fruit and on the following day Magsaysay took his place in the Cabinet. Quirino was compelled to make this appointment because it had become imperative to organize the country against the Huks.

The Hukabalahaps represented the Filipino brand of Communism. The organization had its origins, even as Magsaysay's guerillas, as a movement against the Japanese expansion in the archipelago. Its stronghold was the mountain terrain in the northern parts such as Mindanao. The Huks fought a bitter battle against the Japanese and made it difficult for the foreign imperial power to take root in the nation. After the collapse of the Japanese they set themselves up against the government. They raided for food, killed indiscriminately and were said to be running their own administration, their own schools and their own tax-system. There were constant rumours that they had plans to seize Manila.

The first thing that Magsaysay did after becoming Defence Secretary was to move his department from the Port Area to Camp Murphy. Someone murmured that all the buildings here had already been taken up, but he paid no heed to this. He had a building cleared and moved his department "right away". "Right away" represented the only speed at which he could do things. He was not the kind to allow any time to elapse between the occurrence of an idea and its implementation. He established his office right where the army was stationed. Up till now departmental business had been a long-distance operation between the Secretary and the Commanders.

The army officers, in addition to their usual indifference to a civilian head, viewed the ex-guerilla fighter as an untrained, un-orthodox rabble-leader. But Magsaysay did not wait for their approval in anything that he did. He just stampeded them into respect and obedience. He moved like a tornado in their midst. If he saw them playing poker, when they were on duty, he had them arrested unmindful of who they were. In his whirlwind inspection trips, if he found any of the officers absent from their posts he had them dismissed at once. He transferred those who had lived comfortably in the city back into the country to face the realities of life.

*

Before, the peasantry had as much to fear from the army personnel, posted to guard them, as from the Huks. They had been exploiting their position as saviours and they sometimes squatted on their hosts and demanded all kinds of comforts. Magsaysay made it a rule that army officers should not station themselves on rich land-owners when camping in the country. Within the first six months of his assuming office, he dealt with 300 officers and 3,000 men on various charges of murder, corruption and inefficiency.

He knew that it would be no use merely laying down policies from the secretarial chair if they were to be executed by doubtful personnel. He was perfecting a plan for an all-out change, and "all-out" meant getting even some of the top men out. Castaneda, the Chief of Staff, and Ramos, the Chief of the Constabulary, were notable among those who received his attention. It had not been possible for his predecessor, Kangelon, to dislodge these men, for they were in many ways connected with the President. Kangelon had realized that the Huks were gaining in strength chiefly because of their incompetence and dishonesty. Magsaysay felt that before planning field action against the Huks it was necessary to clean up his own army personnel; but there was a tacit impression everywhere that he would fail in this task.

Ramos was a difficult man to send away. He had been Quirino's classmate and, as Chief of the Constabulary had played a large part in helping him win the election—in fact, as matters stood, the Constabulary's active participation was indispensable for anyone to succeed in the elections. Ramos had command of the special divisions created for fighting the Huks, and, while he did nothing about them, he was active politically, employing the men under him for various purposes. Instead of preparing himself to fight, he was content to play the role of a soothsayer to the President. Quirino often had the satisfaction of hearing from him that internal security conditions were steadily improving. But in this game of soothsaying he went to the extreme once. He gave the President to understand that Taurac, the leader of the Huks had died of tuberculosis. But the joy and relief arising from this good news was shortlived. As soon as the President announced the death of Taurac, he happened to see in *Bahong Buhay*, a Tagolog newspaper, the report of a long interview the editor had had with Taurac. In this interview the Huk leader had experessed the hope that he would, before long, be able to liquidate the unsatisfactory government of Quirino.

Shortly after this, a dastardly murder was committed by the Huks. A party of twelve, including Mrs Quezon (wife of a former President), and her daughter and son-in-law, was set upon by a hundred outlaws and mercilessly machine-gunned. They were on their way to Quezon's birthplace, Baler, where a memorial was to be built for him. President Quirino, who was to preside at the function and who was to be the chief victim of the raid, somehow did not go to the ceremony.

The Huk's reign of terror continued unchecked. They pillaged whole towns, set fire to houses, grabbed whatever they wanted and, when the full force of the Constabulary arrived, disappeared into the mountains again. Often the public was troubled by the Constabulary itself. A report came, about this time, that a hundred persons had been shot and that their houses looted—the culprits were not Huks but members of the Constabulary.

Magsaysay had now a double responsibility on his hands—the task of saving the public from the Huks and also from the Constabulary. First he dealt with Ramos. He issued a circular strictly prohibiting gambling among the army personnel. The penalty was made quite clear—dismissal.

It was known that Ramos held sessions of mahjongg in his house for long periods and collected money from the players. Magsaysay's intelligence service supplied him with factual reports on this and he saw President Quirino and thrust before him the proofs he had collected of Ramos' violations. Quirino tried to belittle the importance of the report, but Magsaysay was so persistent that the President had to agree to his recommendation that Ramos be dismissed.

Magsaysay now turned his attention to Castaneda. This was less easy. Castaneda was a powerful man and it seemed incredible that anyone should try to dislodge him. He had a distinguished record fighting the Japanese and was a graduate of the Philippine Military Academy. He had gone through many spectacular incidents in his life; he once kicked off a hand-grenade thrown on the platform when President Roxas was addressing a gathering. He seemed part and parcel even of the present President. Security arrangements were always thorough under him. It gave an agreeable setting for a Presidential entry and exit to have this imposing man in uniform, with his revolver ever dangling at the waist. It seemed unthinkable that he should ever go or that anyone could have the hardihood to ask him to go.

Magsaysay had now a number of friends in Washington and at the US Embassy in Manila. He arranged for the American Ambassador to meet the President and drop a hint that US aid would depend on army reorganization, now overdue, and that Castaneda should be retired. Magsaysay himself bluntly offered the choice to the President of either keeping Castaneda or being relieved himself. It was a bold gamble on his part, and a dilemma for Quirino, who did not have the courage to say 'Get out' to a man who was promising to redeem the battle-torn country. So he ordered the retirement of Castaneda immediately—the order was signed by the Defence Secretary.

But the Chief of Staff believed that there was some trickery in the order and hoped that Quirino would say if he met him, 'Oh, I never ordered any such thing. It must be Magsaysay's own invention. Throw it in the waste-paper basket.' Both Magsaysay and Castaneda appeared before the President for an unequivocal judgement like the two wives before Solomon. This was a situation that Quirino had not foreseen. And, utterly perplexed, he blurted out that he supported Magsaysay a 100 per cent.

There was a rumour that, in the event of Castaneda being dismissed, there would be mass resignations among the officers. This was not a time to risk an army revolt and Magsaysay wanted to test how he stood with his men. He knew that on a certain day the staff officers were meeting for a discussion of the issue at Camp Murphy. He burst in on the meeting, facing the officers squarely. He had just been starting out to lead a sortie against a group of Huks reported to be in hiding somewhere. He was armed for the expedition, dressed in shorts, and accompanied by armed bodyguards. He asked the officers point-blank whether it was a fact that they intended to resign in sympathy with Castaneda. They were taken aback by the sudden intrusion and by the unexpected manner of his approach. They assured him, as the quickest way to end an embarrassing situation, that the rumour was false. Magsaysay expressed his appreciation of their loyalty and announced that their new chief would be General Ducque.

*

Shuffling and reshuffling, putting a younger man

here, transferring another there, retiring someone of proved stagnation, he prepared his department and the country to face the Huk menace firmly. He judged officers purely on their merit and never allowed either personal regard, social connections or sentiment to affect his decisions. One or two veterans, who had been relieved of their posts, came up to see him with their families and almost showed him their battle scars acquired at Batan or Corregidor. Magsaysay always listened to such appeals with sympathy but never changed his decision. He was particularly hard on those officers who had their commands in remote areas and who had earned a reputation for ill-treating the public.

He attempted to do most of his work by personal inspection and tried to reduce red tape. Often he carried his papers from table to table for sanction of some scheme or for endorsements that were formally needed. He toured all over the Islands by plane, made unannounced trips to various bases and camps, and no one could say when he would descend on a particular place for inspection.

On the very first day of his taking charge as Defence Secretary he had a visitor announced in his office. It was a messenger from one of the Huk leaders—Commander Arthur, who was a relative of José Rizal, the great hero of the nation. President Quirino had no faith in such meetings. He had found that they produced no satisfactory results. Once he had been fooled by the leader of the Huks, Taurac himself.

Commander Arthur had been sending word for a long time, but was heard only on the day Magsaysay became Defence Secretary. Magsaysay drove to the rendezvous which Arthur's messenger had mentioned—a deserted house in Tondo district. Tondo is in the northern part of Manila. Populous, romantically evil-looking and seemingly full of possibilities for dramatic events.

The Commander was waiting at the appointed house. Magsaysay had a two-hour discussion with him on various matters pertaining to the politics and welfare of the nation. He learnt from the Commander that the Communists were arming themselves to overthrow the government. He touched Arthur's pride by referring to his descent from the line of the great Rizal, listened to all that he had to say and then put in his own viewpoint unambiguously.

The result was not seen immediately. They had another meeting a week later at a different rendezvous, in Sampaloc district. There was then a third meeting. At this the young Commander bluntly demanded money to buy a car which he said he badly needed. Without a word Magsaysay gave him 6,000 pesos, not asking for a receipt, out of his secret funds. Several weeks passed. Nothing more was heard of Commander Arthur. Magsaysay was half inclined to believe that he had been fooled like Quirino before and that he would have to write off the amount he had given to the Huk leader.

*

One day the Commander turned up before Magsaysay and announced that he would give him plans for the capture of the chief members of the Huk organization, who lived in Manila under cover. He suggested that they trail a vegetable-seller—a woman—on a certain day, and mark the houses she visited. She was actually not a vegetable-seller, but a despatch-carrier of the Huks. The woman was observed and all the houses she visited were marked. On D-Day, Magsaysay distributed his men all over Manila, armed and ready for action, and rounded up a total of 105 Huks, including all except one covered by Commander Arthur's revelations. But even he was eventually shot in an encounter.

Actually this man had been assigned the job of assassinating Magsaysay at the time of his first meeting with Commander Arthur. But the jeep in which he travelled broke down on the way and by the time he arrived at the rendezvous Magsaysay had gone. This turn of events was perhaps responsible for a change in the mind of Commander Arthur. At his first meeting with Magsaysay he was aware that he was talking to a condemned man, but the fact that Magsaysay survived the meeting must have affected him profoundly and he decided to throw in his lot with him.

Now the brains of the Huk movement had been suppressed and their attack plans and documents seized. This was a tremendous triumph for the Defence Secretary. The President felt gratified about his choice and Magsaysay became a hero in the eyes of the public. It cannot be said that the activities of the Huks ceased altogether after their leaders were rounded up. But this was the first phase of the fight and the authorities had come out successful in it.

Magsaysay now urged the President to suspend the Habeas Corpus Act in respect of cases involving offences such as sedition and political murder. It must be said to Quirino's credit that he had so much faith in his Defence Secretary that he accepted his suggestion and made an immediate pronouncement to the effect, taking upon himself the entire blame and responsibility for the step. It was rather an irony that Magsaysay who fought for democratic principles all his life, should have been instrumental in this democratic lapse. But it must be remembered that he was dealing with a battalion of desperate men. The existing act empowered the police to detain suspects for only six hours. The Huks were dreaded men; if they were freed for a moment, they would certainly resume their violence—the smallest loophole was enough for them to slip through.

After getting the Habeas Corpus Act suspended, Magsaysay turned to organizing the judicial tribunal that was to try the Politburo members. The normal pace of law was unsuited now, for there were a large number of wrongdoers and a sense of urgency was necessary in tackling their cases. Magsaysay employed all his ingenuity to discover means of speedy disposal. Procedural matters and formalities, even if they were inevitable, irked him. He fidgeted while legal experts examined each of the hundred-odd cases and prepared the papers for the prosecution. The

Secretary for Justice found that he could not share his haste, and events moved at their own pace until the middle of 1951, when he resigned. Magsaysay at once recommended the appointment of Justice Castelo to the office and Quirino accepted the advice.

As soon as Castelo took over; events began to move fast and the Defence and Justice departments worked together smoothly. The question arises whether tampering with the machinery of justice was justifiable from any angle and whether it could be defended from an ethical point of view, especially when we remember that Magsaysay was a passionate believer in democracy. It is inconceivable that he could have spent much time brooding over these abstract considerations. He was a man of action; and he was dealing with ruthless men of action; and he wanted to be a match for his opponents. It was a great campaign that he was planning and he wanted to make sure that every detail was contributing to its consummation—the liquidation of the Huk menace.

Yet he never forgot the fact that the Huks were his own countrymen and that they had a right to join any rebellious movement, especially in the context of the misrule prevailing at about this time. And he drew a distinction between those Huks who were in the movement through extraneous causes and those who were just trouble-lovers and anarchists. To wean away the one from the other he intensified the programme started under Roxas and continued under Quirino of offering inducements to the Huks who surrendered to start life anew. The members of the organization were asked either to accept the resettlement programme or face annihilation. There was no room for half measures.

Eventually over 9,000 Huks surrendered and were engaged in the Edcor project (Economic Development Corps)—those killed and captured numbered 12,000. The Edcor farms offered each ex-Huk family six to eight hectares of land. They were given implements, living quarters and seeds. Each unit had its own public amenities. There was a lot of criticism against this scheme and it was said that a Huk received better treatment than a normal peaceable citizen. But Magsaysay's answer was that the Edcor scheme had helped him to deal effectively with at least 50 per cent of the outlaws.

Between January and September 1951, Magsaysay launched a great offensive, starting in the area of Mount Arayat, Pampanga. He drove the Huks from the mountains to the swamps and on to Laguna Bay and thence back to the starting point. He chased them from place to place and soon they were deprived of their hideouts, training grounds and bases. On 29 December, *The New York Times* had reported that the initiative had been wrested from the Huks but that they still constituted a threat. But by about September 1951, it could be said that not only had the initiative passed on to the government but that the Huks were no more a dreaded body.

*

Magsaysay's fame spread far and wide. He was a national hero now and his countrymen looked upon him with love and admiration. Foreigners, particularly Americans, extolled his achievements. People liked to talk about him and think of him as their saviour. He was not averse to all the publicity he received and he watched with interest the image of himself that was gradually taking shape in the public mind. He liked it. He displayed a genius for handling the press. He admitted them at close quarters, hobnobbed with them and put them at their ease. Although there was a separate information section of the army to hand out news, he forestalled it by giving out most of the decisions and activities of his department directly to them.

The Congress sanctioned without a demur an enormous appropriation in the budget under defence—over twice the amount allotted in the days of Kangelon. Some critics said that if Kangelon had been treated as well as Magsaysay in the matter of funds, he might have put down the Huk movement earlier. But such criticism hardly troubled Magsaysay for he knew that his place was secure—in the hearts of the Filipinos.

Three

'Let the President work' was the heading of an

editorial printed on the front page of *The Manila Chronicle,* one week after Magsaysay was sworn in. The subject was rather novel for a press campaign—and it was not that the newspapers were hard up for material. Actually the editorial was addressed not to the President but to the public—it was an appeal to leave him alone. Even a week after he had assumed office, it was still almost impossible for him to find the time or the space to do any work.

He had by an order swept away all the fences and hedges that had grown around men in high positions. One of the first things he did was to throw open the Malacagnan Palace (the Presidential house) to the people. He changed its name to mere Malacagnan (in Spanish, Seat of the Mighty), dropping the 'Palace'. Since the days of the Spanish, it had been a rampart, a symbol of the ruler's might and of his distance from the ruled. After the Spanish, the American heads of government resided here in viceregal splendour. The palace is a huge structure, with heavily framed paintings, red carpets and chandeliers, and baroque decorations. Armed sentries guarded its portals and the public never stepped in.

Now Magsaysay proclaimed that it belonged to the people and that no one should be denied entry. Folks set out from the most distant corners of the archipelago to visit Malacagnan and to speak to their President. At all times the gilded halls were jammed with sightseers. Magsaysay had promised in his election speeches that if he became President he would throw open the palace and the promise was fulfilled now. On the day the President was sworn in there were 80,000 visitors, most of them barefoot or wearing wooden clogs. As many as 10,000 sandwiches and 19,000 bottles of soda were distributed free.

*

Magsaysay invited people to bring to him their grievances. With or without grievances they kept swarming in and out of the palace. As a result the President was often crowded out of his study, finding it extremely difficult to attend to his papers. However averse he was to paper work, he had to get through an inevitable minimum and even this began to pile up.

He announced a new facility to the public. Anyone who had a complaint to make about neglect or corruption could immediately send a free telegram. The resulting deluge of messages was such that the telegraphic communications became choked, and, in a short while, the President had to restrict the facility to messages containing not more than fifty words. Even so he found the task arduous and time-consuming. He remarked: "I have to spend three hours every night reading the mail and telegrams from the people, the poor peasants who have faith in me. No one can do it for me because if the people write to the President, they expect the President to take care of their case."

Sometimes the message of a suffering individual would so upset him that he would abandon whatever he was doing and go out by jeep, plane or car to see things for himself. Romulo in his book has given a description of the President suddenly storming down the staircase and going off somewhere, his aides helplessly waiting to know of his programme and being none the wiser later when they joined him. Magsaysay never waited for others nor did he care for the formalities of drawing up a tour programme. He would set out for the farthest ends of the islands and none would know where he was proceeding until he arrived. His trips were undertaken often to establish some poor barrio family in its rights. A peasant beaten up by his landlord could summon him to find redress. The president would not only go and investigate the matter for himself, but would immediately order the arrest of the landlord if necessary.

An artesian well for every barrio: this was his promise to the people. There were numerous hurdles in the fulfilment of this vision, but he was undeterred by them. He would go out personally to supervise the progress of a well-boring programme—there are photographs of the President standing barefoot in the open, watching with triumph in his eyes a village pump being installed.

He believed that the problem of the nation was a composite of the problems of the smaller people, the unknown, the unnoticed and the obscure. And so the welfare of the country to him meant the welfare of the smallest man. On one occasion, addressing departmental chiefs, he said:

> One thing I want you all to remember. You must pay attention to the little fellow. The big people always manage to take care of themselves. It is your job and mine to take care of the little man.

Not long after assuming office, he declared his personal assets and liabilities. He was always indifferent to questions of money and had the air of having more important things to bother about. But still he insisted on being precise in the matter of announcing his assets and liabilities. He loathed nothing more than acquisitions and his bitterest thoughts were reserved for those who tried to exploit their office or position. He set himself up as an example and soon required of all public servants a declaration of their assets and liabilities. This was the only way by which he could keep a check on corrupt tendencies.

His was a dedicated life and he expected those serving under him to follow his example. He was not unaware of the difficulties that his approach might cause lesser men. He was deeply conscious of human limitations, but still he expected the highest conduct. He said: 'Honesty is not just a badge worn on one's coat-sleeves in a political campaign and then discarded. I have told my people that graft and corruption must be eliminated if the Philippines are to survive and progress. I was elected by an overwhelming vote because I promised to rid the government of the cheats, the crooks and the grafters who threatened our very existence. I am not a superman but a humble person who fully realizes the tremendous responsibilities thrust upon his shoulders. Whatever success I achieve will be with God's help and with the knowledge that I have the Filipino people behind me.' He told the chiefs of the various departments: 'I can promise you this. None of you are going to get rich in your jobs. I know what your assets were when you joined and I know what your assets will be when you leave . . . . When you do leave you are going to be poor, you are going to have grey hair, your face will be lined with wrinkles, and you are going to have a sick body. But you will have served your people well.' He set an example, as always, by greying first.

A month after assuming office, he had to encounter other sources of worry: bickerings and differences among his own men. Major José Crisol, who had been with him as Director of the Psycho-Warfare Branch since the days of his Defence Secretaryship, had violent differences of opinion with Manny Manohan (head of the President's Complaints and Action Committee), and with Castro (Magsaysay's Executive Secretary) over a complaint of extortion by a Chinese resident. The President was then in Baguio, a lovely hill-station which was a four hours' drive from Manila, and he summoned Crisol for a discussion on the subject. Crisol pleaded that he could not make the journey being too busy.

Magsaysay was outraged by this answer and

immediately ordered his dismissal. Such a step did not make him happy, for he had been deeply attached to Crisol. But he still felt it his duty to handle the matter without compunction. He was not one to let his loyalties and personal sentiments swerve him from acting right. After a lapse of time, when his temper had cooled, he called back Crisol and appointed him Under-Secretary for Defence and gave him various other important jobs to do. This has led to the observation by critics that Magsaysay was not really in earnest when he dismissed someone and that he did so for effect after consultation with his would-be victims. But it is difficult to accept such a generalization. Had he acted for effect he would have done many more things to please and impress others and he could have carefully avoided all conflicts with his political associates at various times.

By nature, Magsaysay was not calculating and he always set aside his own loyalties and attachments when deciding on a course of action. This was especially noticeable when he had to deal with his relatives. He respected them and loved them all—his private world consisted of a number of uncles, brothers, brothers-in-law, cousins and so forth. But he made it plain to them that they would receive no special consideration from him. Nietzsche has said that it is not enough that you love your enemies, but that you must actively hate your friends. Magsaysay seemed, at any rate in his office, to follow this dictum. His paternal uncle, Ambrosio Magsaysay, had been given a contract for the transport and supply of coal for a government cement undertaking. The President ordered that this contract be immediately cancelled. He was prevailed upon to consider the matter dispassionately and to take into account the fact that Ambrosio had a good standing as a businessman and that the contract had been settled at the time of Quirino. But such pleas fell on deaf ears and Magsaysay stuck to his decision. Uncle Ambrosio had helped him in his early days, recommending him to Yangco of Try-Tran.

Aurelio Banzon, Luz's elder brother, was Secretary to the Civil Aeronautics Board. He and Magsaysay had been good friends since their schooldays and he had been helpful and co-operative when Magsaysay was courting Luz. Aurelio had reached his present position by dint of his own work and worth and not through his brother-in-law's support. Opening the pages of a newspaper one day in September 1955, Magsaysay was taken aback when he noticed a photograph showing Aurelio attending an aviation meeting at The Hague. Going on official missions abroad was enjoyed by a privileged few and there had been a public outcry against it in the days of Quirino. Magsaysay was determined to put an end to the practice. As a first step, he had issued orders to all departments concerned not to include his relatives in any such delegations. On reading the news item about Aurelio, his first reaction was to thump the table until the paper weights were dislodged. At the following Cabinet meeting he demanded of the Under-Secretary how this had come to pass and on whose authority. It was an explosive scene. The Under-Secretary explained that the President had himself signed the necessary orders. Magsaysay cried that this was a lie and swore that he had never been told of the matter. The Under-Secretary argued again and proved himself in the right. Magsaysay cooled down and muttered that he must have signed without sufficient scrutiny. He suspected that he had been tricked into signing a favour for a relative. The Under-Secretary, now in a state of indignation, offered his letter of resignation; but the President declined to accept it.

In the following November, a similar situation developed between him and his Executive Secretary, Castro. The latter had given him cause for offence in a matter that involved a nephew of Luz Magsaysay. Feliciano de Gala Jr., Luz's elder sister's son, was studying in the United States and needed support in order to pursue his studies. There were exchange limitations and it was not possible to transmit funds from the Philippines, and so it became necessary to devise some other way of helping the boy. He was considered for a small job, carrying a monthly salary of $50, at the Philippine Embassy in Washington. General Vargas, Chief of Staff, blessed the proposal, but on condition that the President also approved it. When the matter came up before Castro, he presumed that the President was already aware of it and eventually sanctioned the appointment in writing. Castro had at that time just returned from a trip to the US and had first-hand knowledge of the case. He also believed that Luz must have already mentioned the subject to her husband. Besides he saw nothing irregular in the appointment since the boy possessed the necessary qualifications and deserved support.

A few weeks later *The Manila Herald* published a report of this appointment along with a comment on nepotism. When Magsaysay read the report, it evoked the expected reaction from him. Castro offered his resignation and the President accepted it. Magsaysay also ordered that any charges debited to the State on account of Gala's trip to Washington and his stay there should be recovered from the boy's parents, if not, from the President's own salary. According to him, purity and truth could not be fragmented. He had an aversion to partial virtues and he felt that one was nepotistic or one was not. Castro was his oldest associate but he had to let him go. Eight months later the President reinstated him, appointing him Judge of the Court of Appeals.

Another case which came dangerously close to his domestic life was that of Gregorio S. Licaros of the Central Bank. Licaros, who was in charge of the import section of the bank, naturally held a position of influence and authority. He was once made Chairman of the Malacagnan Christmas Festival, an organization formed to provide Yuletide joys to poor children. Luz Magsaysay, as the first lady of the land headed it. Licaros raised funds by sending circulars to the business community asking for a quota from among the prosperous importers. Magsaysay learned of it and again reacted as was to be expected. He was furious that his wife's name should be involved in the appeal for funds. He ordered the immediate dismissal of the offending official. The public was aghast at this drastic action. Newspaper editorials pointed out that there was nothing wrong in an appeal in the cause of charity and suggested that the President should act less hastily in such matters. Licaros was a very clear-headed and practical man and his integrity was never in dispute. For a while Magsaysay refused to alter his decision, but after a week he reinstated Licaros.

The President's real struggle now was to establish a tradition and a government according to his long-cherished dreams. Fifteen months after he assumed office, *The New York Times* correspondent wrote:

> When Magsaysay became President in January, 1954, his hair was jet black. Today he is starting to grey at the temples. A Filipino's hair does not start to grey until much later in life.

The President had a variety of problems to face and heavy burdens to carry. First and foremost, he had trouble with the Congress (the legislative house). Every reform bill he proposed hurt someone or the other, and a kind of silent opposition was building up against his most cherished ideas. The members adopted various devices to delay the progress of any bill that they did not like or want, and it was either shelved at the end of a session or so whittled down as to make it ineffective.

Influential members of his own Nacionalista Party disapproved of him silently or even vocally. They were all beginning to realize that the President was no respecter of parties and felt that he had no real place in an organization that they had built up. They could not shake him off now but they derived satisfaction from belittling his intellectual stature and calibre. They quietly chuckled at his lack of sophistication and innocence of outlook and his ignorance of the subtleties of political and public life. Magsaysay for his part felt that they were justified in their contempt and reflected that had he applied himself more earnestly to his education he could have met them now on an equal footing.

*

Guillermo Santos, presiding judge of the Court of Agrarian Relations Commission, was one of the many friends of Magsaysay's whom I interviewed. He had been a specialist in the legal branch of the army until he was appointed Chairman of the Commission. When Magsaysay became President he told Santos: 'I want you. I need you in the Commission.' Santos had still a year to go before completing his full term of twenty years in the army, but Magsaysay would not wait. He said peremptorily: 'Resign your army service and come along.' Santos acted on the advice, because, as he explained, 'The way Magsaysay said it, it left no room for one to doubt, hesitate or think of oneself.' One had to follow Magsaysay's example—he had unreservedly placed his entire self at the disposal of his countrymen and there was no such thing as a set time or hour for his work. At any time of day or night one could call on him. Often he was seen passing orders clad in pyjamas. He would be nervously pacing up and down, muttering, 'All this to be done, all this to be done.'

He could carry on conversations with ten persons at the same time on ten different matters. Santos often wondered whether this was a mere pose or whether Magsaysay really carried in his head the substance of such multifarious talks. He had occasion to test the matter once. When Magsaysay was Defence Secretary he once called up Santos to meet him at Camp Murphy. He was in the midst of a group, but the moment he saw Santos he came up to him and spoke to him for exactly a minute—and to the point—and then he turned back to join the group. He had clear compartments in his mind, and he was brief and precise when he spoke to a man on any subject.

Respect for law was all-important in Magsaysay's eyes. He never let his political supporters get away with their misdeeds. 'Because I was elected by you, don't imagine I am going to stand all your nonsense,' he once said to a landlord who had beaten his tenant. When he was Secretary for Defense, he once received a telegram from the President of the Bar Association in Illolio, complaining about the ill-treatment meted out by an army official to a lawyer held in custody because of his association with the Huks. Santos, who was then a major working in that area, received a telegram from Magsaysay asking him to be ready to join him and go up with him to Illolio. As planned, he set out with Santos, but since no transport was available, stopped a passing jeep—mentioning to the driver who he was—and drove to the lawyer's house. He burst in upon the lawyer's family, busy playing mah-jongg, and started his investigations right away. On completing his inquiry, he ordered the military authorities to treat the man in custody humanely and to allow his lawyers free access to him.

*

Judge Santos took me along on a visit to a barrio. It was within an hour's drive of Manila. The houses were built of timber and they reminded me in a way of the architecture in Kerala. The landscape too had a touch of the Malabar coast. Santos spoke to the villagers and they brought a number of chairs and benches and arranged them for us in open space between the houses. A circle formed around us—elders of the village, wearing picturesque shirts and trousers, some with bare feet, others with wooden shoes.

There was a mobile shop a few yards away selling mashed sweet potato with syrup and ice, and children came running and swarmed around the woman vendor. Two mongrels growled and chased each other. From where we sat, I could glimpse the interior of the houses—they looked tidy with their simple furniture and curtains.

Young men leaned over the railings of their houses and watched us with a smile. They said nothing, the elders did the talking. Santos asked them a few questions on Magsaysay and interpreted the answers. Magsaysay had given them a feeling of belonging. He had listened to their problems and understood them immediately. This barrio had voted for his rivals, still he had come here and attended to their needs. When asked to say something critical of Magsaysay, one of the villagers remarked that his only complaint was that the former President was too careless. As the head of a nation he should never have gone out without a proper escort. It had been perhaps thanks to this carelessness that he lost his life.

1960

PERMITTED LAUGHTER*

I SUPPOSE ONE MAY NOW LOOK BACK WITH RELIEF on the passing of a phase of our existence when every journalist in the country was menaced or manacled unless he wrote what he plainly saw was nonsense or, worse, untruth. Day after day the editor, the publisher and the feature writer had to hold their breath and await directions from an individual who might be decent and intelligent in private life, but who had to function as

* 'A ban on cartoons amounts to a ban on laughter.' The writer describes the dismal days when his brother, R. K. Laxman, had to run with his cartoons to get them cleared by the censor. And how innocuous were the ones which were banned!

a censor and could survive only by a show of extreme mindlessness and pugnacity.

A deadly monotony had seized our newspapers and the distinction between one newspaper and another was lost. All papers and journals sounded alike, as if they had been drilled to sing in a chorus. But the reader would not be taken in—he glanced down the column mechanically and distrusted every word in it. Even such a serious matter as shots being fired at a candidate during an election campaign left him unmoved and he just commented, 'Oh, it is just another piece of fiction put out for some purpose. Wait till tomorrow and you will know why.' The average citizen was convinced that day by day he was being fed on exaggeration, half-truths, quarter-truths and mini-truths, if not lies; and he steeled himself against their influence.

*

Those who were responsible for this unholy situation, however, fell victims to their own falsehoods. Into the citadel of authority no other kind of report penetrated except what they liked to hear, often a feedback of the stuff they themselves had generated.

In ancient times, as the dramatists have presented it to us, it was not unusual for a king to question his minister from time to time without putting even his nose out of the window: 'Are we getting three rains a month unfailingly?'

'Yes, of course, Your Majesty.'

'Our subjects continue to be contented and loyal?'

'Yes, undoubtedly, Your Majesty.' Whereupon the king switched his mind off State matters and returned to his domestic pursuits. An extreme instance of this condition I read about in history: One Ganga Raja, ruler of Sivasamudram in AD 16, was playing chess in the harem and casually enquired what the uproar that reached his ears meant, and was told by his minister, 'Oh, a lot of noisy children are playing outside the palace gate.' The king continued his chess game until the insurgents reached his chamber and cut short his chess game as well as his career.

What a censor will not realize is that truth cannot be kept hermetically sealed under a lid. It will be out in all sorts of unexpected ways like a blob of mercury pressed under one's thumb.

It was in the above context that I viewed Laxman's cartoons, banned during the Emergency, bearing out my hopeful statement to him in the dismal days that he would survive his censor.

1977

REFLECTIONS ON FRANKFURT

TO ME THE WORD 'FAIR' GENERALLY CONJURES up a vision of sprawling sheds in a field, blinding illuminations, deafening announcements from loudspeakers, dust, bustle and congestion. I had imagined books, instead of cosmetics and gewgaws, displayed in a similar background in Frankfurt also.

'Where is the Fair?' I had asked, though standing in front of the permanent exhibition buildings—mansions in several blocks to accommodate about 8,000 booksellers and publishers representing over 120 countries, and with enough space for a total of 1,00,000 visitors to move around freely.

Ice-cream, coffee and snacks available at every corner, to mitigate the fatigue of rambling and browsing in this vast universe. One's feet and legs protest and grow heavy in spite of the facilities provided for movement with a free continuous shuttle service between the buildings, and escalators and mobile belts within the halls themselves.

Preceding the formal opening of the book fair, meetings of Indian authors and publishers were held at the City Hall auditorium where one heard recitations, readings and discussions. On the whole, academic in tone, except when authors complained against their publishers on the subject of royalty and payments, and the publishers in their turn spoke of the difficulties they experienced from suspicious writers. Mrs Kamala Das said that her best-selling book in English never brought her adequate returns, although her publisher a few moments earlier had in his speech claimed her as their best-selling author. Ms Qurratulain Hyder, eminent Urdu writer, said that her books have been selling in India and all neighbouring countries in thousands for a quarter of a century now, but her publishers never paid her any royalty; they brought out new editions of her works under different imprints and pretended they were pirated editions.

Another speaker held the audience spellbound with a blistering attack on the Sahitya Akademi with which he had been associated officially for years. There was much justice and logic in what he said, but the general feeling was that this was not the occasion nor place to expose our weak points and failures.

Equally outrageous was the speech by a lady, one of the guests from India, at the podium where she was expected to speak on tradition and change or some such theme. While the speakers who preceded her confined themselves to the subject, our lady commenced her speech with, 'Friends and Germans.' One almost expected her to say, 'I've come to bury Caesar, not to praise him.' She almost fulfilled this expectation by launching on a tirade against the German character. According to her, all Germans were unfriendly, grim and unsmiling, whereas the Indian tradition was to smile and greet and show hospitality to all strangers. The speaker suggested that the German Government would do well to appoint official smilers on a salary of DM 1,000, whose only business would be to stand in street corners and keep smiling. Finally, she wailed: 'All I am asking for is love from Germans.' We felt embarrassed as this was an extravagant demand and her attack totally unwarranted, since we had experienced nothing but royal hospitality and kindness from our hosts. We were put up in excellent hotels, provided with transport and with every comfort one could want.

*

I heard rumours in Frankfurt and then in Paris and London that I was to be awarded the Nobel Prize this year(1986). Some Paris newspapers carried the 'short-listed' names of three writers in the Third World, as the committee had decided to award the Prize to the Third World this year to overcome the charge of being biased in favour of American and European writers. I was greeted and congratulated here and there. I could not be sure this honour would be welcome at this stage of my life. I had mixed feelings about it. I am already a victim of excessive public attention. Frankly, I feel uneasy (and angry) when cameras are pointed at me, and try to avoid interviews, greetings, and attempted 'felicitations,' and above all unnecessary correspondence. I love to be left alone and not noticed whatever reception my writing might have. And the prospect of becoming a 'laureate' was nightmarish. Thank God, it passed.

If my name actually did come up, and then was dropped, I speculate on the arguments one might have overheard from the committee room before the decision on 16 October.

'For half a century Narayan has been building up a world of his own and peopled it with a variety of characters, who have ceased to be fictional, but are recognized and loved in any part of the world by Narayan's readers . . . it is an achievement which should be treated as a contribution to world literature,' argued one.

'To a certain extent, yes,' said the arbiter. 'This author's work is diverting, amusing and readable, but possesses none of the elements that go to make great literature.'

'What are those elements of great literature?'

'All great literature must echo the soul of man. The struggles, agonies and anguish in the soul of the individual must be reflected in the work, against the background of historical and social convulsions of the countries in which the individual finds himself tossed about as a helpless victim. All the grimness of existence must find a place in a writer's work. Above all, a certain degree of obscurity and difficulty of idiom in the text enhances the stature of a literary work.

'Applying these tests, Narayan's work fails. His writing is too simple, and too readable, requiring no effort on the part of the reader. Mere readability is not enough. A reader must be put to work and must labour hard to get at the meaning of a sentence; only then can he feel triumphant at having mastered a page.

'Narayan's further defect lies in his light-hearted tone under all circumstances. This is a grave defect. Humour is all very well up to a point, but it is not everything in literature. Humour has a tendency to stimulate frivolity. Our Founder and Benefactor, Alfred Nobel, you must remember, invented the dynamite, which is no joke, and it would be inappropriate to award the prize in his name to a writer who is uncommitted to the serious and sinister problems of existence.

'Narayan has produced quite a body of work to fill up bookshelves and shows promise. He has created a new map called Malgudi in which his characters live and die. Story after story is set in the same place, which is not progressive, a rather stagnant background. Narayan's stories fail to reflect the dynamism of India's civilization or aspirations.

'We hope some day Narayan will develop into a full-fledged writer deserving our serious consideration.'

1986

VAYUDOOT

VAYUDOOT IS MUCH IN THE NEWS TODAY. TWO years ago I had the honour of inaugurating the service at Mysore with garland, speech, tea and biscuit. The inauguration was spectacular but the arrangements for the flight seemed casual and unconvincing. There was no sort of runway within sight—only a grass field with cattle grazing peacefully, around a little cottage which is called 'Mandakalli Aerodrome' and which resembles a one-roomed forest inspection bungalow, with a tiny toilet in a corner. We the citizens of Mysore have been agitating for over three decades for an 'adult' airport. We have put forth excellent reasons why Mysore should be included in the air map: every week Mysore receives several thousand visitors and tourists, who come by bus or train, and Mysore is a venue for frequent conferences, meetings, seminars and academic activities—these and other reasons are reiterated from time to time by august bodies such as the Chamber of Commerce, Rotary, the Lions, City Corporation, and so on, but without effect. 'Mandakalli' remains what it was thirty-five years ago.

The Dornier can take in only eighteen passengers at a time, but the congregation has the appearance of a milling crowd in the mini-hall, with all kinds of make-shift arrangements for checking in the passengers. The tiny toilet at the corner serves for security-checking of women passengers, while the men are frisked and searched before an assembly of onlookers.

After the speeches and photographs we march towards the Dornier, which is sitting prettily on the grass field, white and looking like a magnificent cow grazing. We climb a couple of steps grasping a rope for hand-rail, and occupy our seats. So far all is well and comfortable—until the engine is started and that seems to be the end of one's auditory facilities. I have never experienced such a monstrous assault on my eardrums before or after. I have no choice but to bear it until we land in Bangalore after thirty minutes. For more than ten days, the tremor of my eardrums persisted, necessitating several visits to an ear specialist. Later I wrote a detailed letter to the Minister for Civil Aviation of my experience in the Dornier. Perhaps we were on the threshold of a brand new National Malady: 'Dornier Syndrome'.

Days passed, but there was no sign of an acknowledgement from the Minister. I was not surprised, but felt guilty of squandering a couple of hundred words which I could have put to better use professionally.

Later at Parliament, I came face to face with Mr Jagdish Tytler and mentioned my letter to him so far remaining unacknowledged. He had no idea of what I was talking about. I repeated the essential part of my letter wherein I had suggested that while they were at it, they should make the Dornier cabin soundproof in order to save our ears. He showed no symptom of following my speech; I thought I was mumbling inaudibly and wondered whether I should raise my *sruti.* While I was speculating thus, he turned on his heel and vanished.

The Dornier stands cleared by the Safety Board—now, as it seems, to the extent of assuring us that the door will not fall off again in mid-air, as it happened during a flight from Delhi.

As far as I am concerned, I decided that my inaugural flight in a Dornier would be my final one too, when I heard that after the inauguration ceremony the service had to be suspended for some days, owing to the engine catching fire in one place, the propeller getting out of commission another time, when according to rumours, a poor loader got entangled in it, and some other mishap another day. Fortunately the mishaps and snags occur only on the ground, and not at 7,000 feet. Perhaps that is what the Safety Board's certificate means!

1987

THE ENEMIES

WE ARE IN THE HABIT OF HONOURING THE memory of personalities who have served society in some role or other—patriots, poets, scientists, engineers, inventors, saints, composers and so on, and who have deepened and enriched human experience in different ways. I was once in a committee of All India Radio, the agenda at a particular meeting being to commemorate regularly the services and achievements of national heroes. As a first step we tried to compile a list of names, and realized soon that we had before us over six hundred names to honour, which meant six hundred hours of broadcasting even if we allotted one hour a day for this programme. The proposal seemed unpractical and was turned over to the care of a sub-committee and was lost sight of.

Later my thoughts proceeded in another direction. Why not compile a directory of enemies of society? This enemy does not rob or shoot, but invents something which causes damage and destruction, unintentionally though. For example, the man who first got the idea of polishing floor tiles created a disastrous fashion, a potential cause of damage and misery. The biped is precariously balanced on two slender supports, which have to bear an increasing load as one grows older. In childhood one keeps tumbling a great deal but recovers quickly from bruises on elbows and knees, but the adult whose foot slips cannot recover so easily, and then at an advanced age even a slight skidding may prove deadly. Observe an orthopaedic clinic, and you will have an idea of the number of fractures of hips and thighs that occur each day, after a fall mostly in a bathroom. It is suicidal to polish the bathroom floor and to fit therein a shiny porcelain bathtub in which you will have to progress at the pace of a tight-rope walker. I remember the instance of the missing host when the *griha pravesam* ceremony was in full swing in a new house. He had skidded while emerging from the tornado shower over the bathtub. The bathroom door was ultimately broken open and the master of ceremonies rescued. We need not go into unhappy details, but suffice to say that he was immobilized for a year. A dazzling bathtub and a mirror-finish flooring are a deadly combination. It is surprising that those who build fashionable houses prefer to live dangerously all life. I hear frequently, 'Everything is ready, but for the floor-polisher who is delaying . . . .' When I hear that I feel like bursting out, 'Keep him off please, for heaven's sake, and may your limbs and joints remain intact when you come to live in your new home.'

Now to turn to another kind of enemy: he does not contrive to trip you up, but tries to destroy you from the top by shattering your eardrums. In this category the inventor of the air horn must take the first place. If I have to erect a statue in order to demolish it later to mark my protest, I'd choose the inventor of the air horn for the honour. It is the least wanted invention at a time when we seem to be seeking protection from 'noise' all day, in all places. No invention is more uninvited and pernicious. The damage it does to your eardrums is incalculable. When a bus or lorry screams past one's path or at one's rear while driving, the noise attacks, shatters, squashes and deprives one of all judgement and paralyses all thought and conversation and concentration; and it takes quarter of an hour at least to recover from its effects, and then comes along the next one screaming off the previous one, and so on in a succession.

Young men who pull out the silencer from their motorcycles must also be enrolled in the blacklist. There are enough laws and regulations to prohibit all such evil, but they are not enforced in our tolerant society.

The man who invented the loudspeaker must also go into the blacklist. One is thankful for the police regulation in Madras banning trumpet speakers through which organizers of ceremonials spread film music and political harangue night and day, sometimes far into the night. When the suppliers of loudspeakers went on a strike for a day recently as a protest, no strike was more welcome. One felt like shouting, 'Keep it up for ever.'

1987

ON LANGUAGE

AT DELHI I MET A MAN WHO COMPLAINED, 'I'M just back from Madras after a visit, and there I found to my shock, they do not receive the Hindi news on Doordarshan, but only Tamil news from the Madras kendra at 8.40 p.m! Who permitted this and why?'

'For the reason that Hindi is not understood in that part of the country.'

'How can you say that? It's unconstitutional to avoid Hindi. Such unconstitutional practices must be discouraged.'

'It seems that the Chief Minister desired that Tamil news should be telecast at that hour.'

'Oh! Oh! Chief Minister indeed! If we go on

consulting every Chief Minister's wish, we will get nowhere.'

'But I repeat, Hindi is not understood in Madras.'

'How can it not be understood while it is written down in the constitution as the official language?'

'You may give a man an excellent cookery book, but it will not help if he has not learnt how to cook.'

'What cookery book? In Hindi or English?'

'What does it matter?'

'If it is in Hindi, he must understand it.'

'It's probably in English.'

'English can have no place in our country. It is not in the Eighth Schedule.'

'Whatever you may say, Hindi is not understood, and whatever is not understood remains ununderstood . . . . It is axiomatic, you cannot escape it.'

'Hindi is easy to learn. No axiom in it, whatever it means.'

'You may shout your message in Hindi through a loudspeaker, but it will make no sense to one who is deaf to it.'

'It seems to me just perversity. Hindi is easy to learn, a gentle language.'

'I agree it is a gentle language, but being promoted in ungentle ways.'

'Why won't you people of the south accept it?'

'Listen. Because of champions like you, who assume a dictatorial tone and decree must and must not for others. Your tone is self-defeating, counterproductive. While the old caste system is condemned, you are displaying a new caste-superiority and preen yourselves before non-Hindi folk and attempt to order them about, which looks comical. You will have to mend your manners. Approach us normally, with humility, if you wish to achieve results. If you remember, there was a time when in most south Indian homes there were at least a couple of members who attended Hindi classes and appeared for examinations voluntarily, but all that stopped the moment the order came from Delhi that everyone should know Hindi as the only language. It is a historical fact. Think it over. There is still a chance that we shall attain national integration. Good-bye till then.

'Before you go I want to compliment you on your excellent English. Keep it up, otherwise we could not have exchanged ideas. You would perhaps have gone on in Hindi and I would have been eloquent in Tamil. The situation would have been similar to the one in my story in which a travelling American and a villager he encountered on the roadside carry on a prolonged dialogue in perfect American-English and impeccable local dialect respectively . . . . The American thought he was making an offer for a life-size clay horse, in whose shade the villager was resting, and the villager thought the foreigner was eager to buy the two goats he owned which were grazing nearby . . . . Well, why don't you read the story yourself unless you have made a vow not to look at an English sentence.'

1988

TALE OF A TUB

WHY DID DIOGENES, THE GREEK PHILOSOPHER live in a tub? (Some say it was a barrel, whatever it might have been he lived in a very constricted space. I have often wondered why.) I have the answer now because he could not get out of the tub, as I myself realized recently when I stepped into a bath and could not rise from it.

I had just arrived at my hotel in London and within an hour of unpacking, I thought it'd be nice to start the season with a warm bath in the deep blue tub, which caught my attention the moment I peeped into the bathroom. My granddaughter, Minnie, warned me from another bathroom, 'Wait till I finish. There is no shower in that bathroom.' I respected her warning for ten minutes and said to myself. 'What if there is no shower? A good dip in this glorious blue tub is worth all the shower in the world . . . .'

I was reckless and wanted to prove I was wiser to prefer a blue tub bath and to surprise her when she emerged from her shower and found me all spruced up after the overnight flight from India, ready to go out. I should have been more observant and realized that the sapphire-blue tub was enormous. It was probably an antique designed for Henry the Eighth. It was so deep that I could not step into it except through special manoeuvres, first sitting on the edge and carefully lowering myself in by stages.

I had, however, the good sense not to turn on the taps except partially, the only precaution in an otherwise senseless adventure. If the taps had flowed freely, I should have drowned. Fortunately, the water level came up only a few inches and was just enough to wet my back, chest and ankles.

Presently when I wanted to get up and out of it, I realized I could not. The walls of the tub proved slippery. There was no sort of handle anywhere. I could not kick against the wall of the tub and get up, since the tub was over ten feet in length and my feet could not touch the end. I desperately tried to lift myself in any manner possible but always slipped back supine, but I took care not to hit my head on the projecting taps. I made several more attempts and gave up. I thought my end had come. If none noticed my absence, I could lie there starving and soaked to the skin till doomsday. As a last resort, I screamed 'Minnie!' although I doubted if I could be heard from that cavernous tub.

Luckily for me, Minnie heard and was soon at my door, bolted on my side. 'I can't open the door! Why have you bolted it? Dry yourself and come out. Have you got a towel?' she asked. 'I see a towel but it is out of my reach. I am not able to get up from the tub. I keep slipping back. I may crack my spine or hips or ankles unless I lie still. If I make the slightest movement, I am dragged back. I do not know what to do. I have no clothes on and am shivering . . . .' Very soon the full family had assembled at the door and were crying out encouraging, cheering words to keep up my morale.

'Can't you somehow reach the bolt and draw it open?'

'If I could leave this blasted tub—I would come out of this hell like a whirlwind and do many things.'

They went down to the reception and brought help. I could hear a pneumatic drill operating at the door for what seemed an eternity, and a chunk of the door cut away with the bolt since it had tightly lodged in and could not be shaken. The door smashed open.

Presently a gigantic mechanic stood over my tub and said, 'Here, take my hand and come out . . . .'

'I can't—my joints are stiff . . . .'

Finally, he bent low and turned his back to me, so that I could encircle my arms around his neck and cling to his back while he just lifted me off like a sack and put me on dry land.

1990

TEACHING IN TEXAS

A TEACHER FEELS PROUD WHEN HE FINDS AN occasion to say, 'So and so is (or was) my student.' It is not important what sort of a teacher he might have been—whether a sadist or an inoffensive kind. Whatever the type, he feels an inner glow when uttering the magic phrase '*My* student'.

I enjoyed the luxury of this sentiment for four months when I spent a semester as a visiting Professor at Austin, University of Texas. When I received the proposal first it seemed impossible since I do not have the scholarship or the discipline required for the task. But the offer was attractive and I love to visit America on any excuse. Formerly, at different times, I had visited four universities as a Distinguished

Visiting Professor, but that was different. On those occasions only my 'distinguished' presence was required, one lecture and a couple of informal sessions with students now and then, but no routine task.

But now at Austin I was being employed as a member of the faculty with specific duties. I felt rather frightened. I had to talk on subjects such as 'Religion and Caste in the Indian Novel' to the undergraduates and 'Indian Writing in English' to graduates. It took me time to understand that 'graduate' meant our 'post-graduate' and 'undergraduate' meant our 'graduate' or BA level. Following my acceptance I was asked to formulate courses of study for both the classes. Also I was asked to produce a special list of 'recommended reading' and 'required reading' for the students. I was again puzzled.

I had never been too methodical in my reading, though at one time I pored over a simple 'Outline of English Literature' and attempted to read a couple of books from each literary period—plays, poems and essays—starting with Chaucer. After that I read whatever came my way including literary periodicals such as *The Times Literary Supplement, John O'London's Weekly* and *T. P.'s Weekly, Bookman, Encounter, London Mercury,* purely for pleasure without any aim or purpose. Now to prescribe material for academic purposes seemed a terrific responsibility. Also they wanted the lists immediately to enable them to order books well in advance of my arrival.

With the help of a friend, I managed to send off

through fax an imposing list of books, which included some of my own. I had had a brainwave at the last minute to suggest in one of my letters:

> I wonder if I may teach my own novels and short stories, explaining their genesis and my technique of utilizing the material I gather from my own surrounding, as the main course.

It seemed to me more practical than plodding through other writers and interpreting them. Dr Lariviere, Director of the Asia Center, welcomed my idea with the rider that I should include one or two other Indian writers for comparative study as required by the university regulations. So I added to my list Mulk Raj Anand's *Coolie* and *Untouchable,* Raja Rao's *Kanthapura,* U. R. Ananthamurthy's *Samskara,* and Anita Desai, and managed to draft courses of study for both the classes.

Although I had never read any book with the purpose of extracting any philosophical or social meaning, now in a classroom, when I started talking about a novel or a story, I discovered new dimensions in it, apart from character, incidents and construction. I elaborated the theory that there could be no such thing as *absolute* fiction; any fiction must have its source (even if it is not visible at first sight to the naked eye), in some pattern of life, whether you call it fable, allegory, ballad, or cock-and-bull story. I developed this theory in the classroom day after day, the inspiration being the young eager listeners looking up to me for knowledge and noting down faithfully every word.

The teacher's chair exercised its own magic—like the throne of Vikramaditya of our legends. Even an idiot spoke inspiredly when he ascended its thirty-two steps and occupied the seat, although when he came down, he was again dumb and dull. So from my seat I explained the evolution of 'The Caste System in India' and spoke of 'untouchability' although the phrase sounded, as I explained, absurd (there being no such word as 'touchability'). But the term somehow came into existence in Indian society, till Mahatma Gandhi made it his mission in life to fight it and banned the term 'untouchables', whom he called instead 'Harijans', meaning 'God's children'.

After this preamble lasting a couple of days, the story of *Untouchable* by Mulk Raj Anand made sense to the student who read the novel and came back the following week well prepared, asked questions, and wrote papers on the theme in its various aspects, based on the novel.

To complete the picture of the caste system at the other extreme I took up Ananthamurthy's *Samskara,* which describes high-caste orthodox Brahmin society, with its rigours and taboos, in a plague-ridden mountain village in Karnataka province. In between, I explained, there lay whole gradations of social order, which formed the framework of the caste system. (Naranappa, a Brahmin cast out of society for his apostatic ways—drinking, meat-eating, and associating with low-class women—dies suddenly, and his body lies in an untouchable colony. The whole village is exercised over the question as to who should dispose of the body and how. Many Shastras are scrutinized by the leader of the community, and orthodox committee meetings are held, while the body is rotting. Finally, an untouchable woman who loved him takes charge of the body and arranges for its cremation.)

There are many subtle points of sociological interest in the story, which gave much scope for discussion in the class. Out of it came a number of papers the students wrote on the theme. This was again followed by questions, and then discussion among the students themselves. I could judge the result of my method from the papers they submitted from time to time, choosing the themes themselves from the text. I found the papers edifying and could gauge the kind of impact a serious novel could have on a reader with an enquiring mind.

I recommended also three of my own novels and several short stories. I had never imagined the existence of any social, ethical and philosophical implications in my stories till the students called them out and debated among themselves, and then chose the themes for their papers. I had warned them from time to time, 'Because I am the author sitting here, explaining my own work, a rather unusual situation, please don't hesitate to attack the book and the author as frankly as you please.' Thus I had to face and parry remarks such as, 'You have made Rosie in *The Guide* guilty of adultery. Couldn't she have remained chaste and faithful to her husband and still pursue her art? Do you approve of adultery?' 'Why are the women characters in your stories so spineless?' 'Is the wife in *Dark Room* a typical Indian wife? She seems to be only a slave of Ramani, not his wife.' 'In *Malgudi Days*, your stories are all about down-and-out persons. Why didn't you choose to write about better lives?'

I would give some reply which came to my mind on the spot, and which might be rejected by one and accepted by another and result in a seminar with several points of view emerging. This would go on for three hours, as on Mondays I had to steer the graduates through a three-hour period. When it was proposed, I resisted the idea. 'How can I lecture for three hours? It will exhaust me. I can't speak for three long hours. I am used to radio broadcasting and such, which take up less than twenty minutes—less than 2,000 words if I wrote them beforehand.' Lariviere was very tolerant. He said, 'For this particular hour on Monday you may have to speak for fifteen minutes just to initiate a subject and then you will find that it develops into a seminar with the whole class participating and managing it. You will find three hours gone without your noticing it.' He was right.

I found this particular Monday session engrossing and rewarding while I just watched and listened between three and six in the afternoon. Lariviere had said to me earlier in his letters, 'Ours is only a suggestion. Nothing is rigid, remember. You may develop the courses and your teaching method as you think fit.' It was this kind of elasticity and absence of bureaucratic rule that charmed me most. I was also given the choice of either holding a final examination or not for the graduates. I had graded their papers from time to time and saw no reason to hold a final examination. In the last week when I announced, 'No examinations,' I received thundering cheers from the whole class, while realizing thereby my life-long ambition to abolish the examination system, and all the unnecessary tension that kills the joy of living in young people.

1991

ON WALKING

I HAVE BEEN ALL MY LIFE A WALKER. I USED TO walk along the tree-shaded trunk road leading out of the city of Mysore, in every direction, on the roads leading to the forests of Bandipur or Karapur, from my home in Laxmipuram, or amble along the base of Chamundi hill through rugged paths, reach Lalitha Mahal Palace on the East horizon and return home—after nearly five hours of walking, brooding, thinking and making plans for my future or my writing, usually on weekends or during those years when I failed in my exams and studied privately, without having to attend classes, for next year's chance (which I considered a blessed state as it left me in a state of unalloyed freedom).

My father, though a disciplinarian and a strict headmaster of our High School, did not mind what I did; he didn't have faith in the educational system. He left me free to read whatever I liked out of the school library. Wandering about morning and evening, I felt intoxicated by the charms of nature. The air was clean and pure, avenue trees were in bloom. Evening I walked about two or three miles around the Kukara Halli Tank, listened to the soft splash of wavelets on the shore and watched the display of colours in the western sky. I do not mind repeating what I have said earlier in my essays, that the sunset in Mysore is unique and not seen anywhere else in the world.

I went round the tank and then sat on a bench on the bund. A little farther off on another bench, I could see Venkatappa, a distinguished artist of Mysore who arrived at about 4:30 in the afternoon every day and watched the sky all evening, well past the dusk, and then rose to go. He wore a white dhoti and a coat over it, crowned with a turban; an umbrella was tucked under his arm in all seasons. He sought no company, was content to commune with the sky till the last splash of colour vanished.

He was a bachelor and a recluse, was dedicated to painting, a genius who sought no patrons or admirers, a totally self-contained man. He has left several water-colours, paintings which are to be seen at the Jagan Mohan Palace Gallery and at Bangalore. He had a few friends who were on visiting terms and who saw his pictures in progress and listened to his veena, as he was also devoted to music. I am straying away from my original theme, which was walking, and which includes landscape, which in turn includes stars and the sky and the lake and Venkatappa rapt in watching the wonderful spectacles. People knew him only at a distance, which he maintained all through life. Though considered a recluse, it seems to me he was more hermit-like.

At sunset I too moved; cobras were said to crawl out of the crevices in the pile of rugged stone forming the bund. I walked to the market-place to jostle with the crowd. In all, morning and evening, I must have walked ten miles a day without any reckoning or purpose in walking. I walked because I enjoyed it and had the leisure. While walking, my mind became active and helped my writing.

I kept up this pace for years wherever I happened to be—although nature was not the same everywhere as in Mysore. That charm and the abandon could not normally continue owing to new responsibilities and changing routine, but I continued my walking as a habit wherever I might be—until last year when I fell ill and had to stay in a hospital for a few weeks. When my condition improved, I was permitted to walk again in regulated doses. 'You may walk up to that cottage Number 24, with the nurse's help . . . .' And then, 'Be sure to walk for ten minutes exactly, from your bedroom to the hall in your home.' As I progressed, I was permitted more time—thirty or forty minutes in the park. I have lost the habit of walking in the street, dodging the scooters and autorickshaws and the potholes and pitfalls so strictly preserved by the Corporation. Nowadays, I walk in the park near my home both in Madras and Mysore, arriving there in my car.

The park is a world in itself. Here you see a variety of motives in operation. The men who walk for athletic reasons, not a few, seem to be in training for the Olympics. Jogging, running, with upraised arms or swinging them in windmill fashion, stopping in their tracks to bend down, stretch or kick imaginary balls, jumping high and low, with not a care for others in their path. For me these Human Windmills are a terror.

Those who are here on medical advice are easily spotted from the style by which they carry themselves, pushing forward as if punishing themselves for all the years of stagnation and neglect. Some of them walk as if chased by a tiger, heaving, panting and perspiring. The doctor must have advised, 'Take a brisk walk, don't slouch or amble long.' And they practice an unaccustomed exercise. There is always a group of older men seated on the bench on the lawn, perhaps *vanaprasthas,* talking of old times and current politics and comparing one another's health.

Young couples sitting in remote corners, in the shelter of bushes, conversing in whispers, their backs turned to the public. Day after day they sit there, I get very curious to know what they are saying. Of course, there must be an affirmation of each other's dedication, devotion. It can't go on repeated a thousand times day after day ad nauseam. They must have other things to talk about: their homes and parents or the hurdles in their way.

I would give anything to understand them, I wish them well and success to their romance. I know the whispers will cease ultimately, once they become man and wife. You can't go on whispering all life. There will come a natural phase when you will shout at each other in the course of an argument or spend long pauses of silence, sitting in two chairs and staring ahead at a wall, a tree, with no subject left for conversation. All that could be said has been said, followed by an unmitigated, pregnant silence. A perfect attunement and communication of minds has been attained where speech is superfluous. In Kamban's *Ramayana*, when Rama and Sita are left alone after the wedding, they remain silent, having nothing to say. The poet explains, 'Those who were always together eternally as Vishnu and Lakshmi and separated only a moment ago have no need to talk.'

A couple come and part at the gate and move in opposite directions without uttering a word, reminding me of Byron's line: 'When we two parted in silence and tears.' Fresh young couples are however cheerful and relaxed, commenting on flowers and plants and smiling all through, especially if they have a toddler with them.

Students sit in little groups here and there. Cheerless and grim, anxiety writ large on their faces, desperately making up for wasted months. I sometimes enquire what they are studying and what their hopes are. They do not seem to mind the disturbance. Sometimes I ask to see the book in their hands. They are always glad to be interrupted. Last week I looked through a book that they were trying to 'mug up'. It was a bazaar 'guide' to English Prose for BA. Leafing through I found my name listed in the contents with two stories included. The stories were paraphrased, annotated in Tamil and summarized in English.

Two thousand words of my composition reduced to twenty words expertly, with definitions of 'difficult' phrases and possible questions and answers. The young men, the examinees, found this tabloid presentation more clear-headed and acceptable than the original. With these, they might also attain a First Class in English. I wondered for a moment if I should declare my authorship of the two stories, but I returned the glorious guide to them and passed on, not being sure if they could bear to see a live author and also because I was not sure I could answer if they questioned me on my stories, as they were likely to be more up-to-date with the subject.

1992

ON VED MEHTA

SOME YEARS AGO VED MEHTA, (OUR distinguished man of letters, settled in New York) was almost my neighbour when I occupied an apartment on East 57th Street. He was on East 58th Street. He was planning a profile of me for the *New Yorker* magazine, which brought us together. When we met he would gather information and biographical data about me unobtrusively. He had lost his vision when he was three years old through an attack of meningitis. When he was fifteen, he was sent to the Arkansas State School for the Blind, where he was trained to develop alternative faculties such as touch and hearing and memory. He benefited from his schooling to such an extent that he was able to pursue an academic career, with distinction both in America and England. In his company one never noticed his handicap. He moved about freely without carrying a white walking-stick. He managed to gather details of my life day by day, in a subtle manner without obvious questioning, and in due course produced a ten-thousand-word masterpiece entitled 'The Train Arrived in Malgudi' for the *New Yorker* (later included in his collection of essays, *Johnny is Easy to Please*).

He was uncannily sensitive and alert. In those days I was addicted to chewing betel-nut and carried a stock in a little tin container. Once when I took it out of my pocket, he asked, 'Narayan, what is that rattling noise?' I handed him the tin box. He ran a finger lightly over it to gauge its dimensions and asked, 'What colour is it?' sniffed its contents, remarked, 'Spiced with cardamom and cloves, I suppose,' and returned it to me. Later, I found my addiction described in his essay, with the size and colour of the little tin container mentioned.

While crossing a street he stopped on the edge of the kerb when the 'Don't Walk' sign came on. He explained to me that he was guided by the vibrations he felt underfoot when others walked or stopped! Whenever I visited his apartment, he offered me coffee after warning me not to follow him into the kitchen. In fifteen minutes he would emerge with a tray of coffee and toast. The articles in his kitchen were arranged with such mathematical precision that by stretching out his hand he could pick up whatever he needed—coffee-maker, marmalade, toaster, cutlery, cups and other things, and he knew also the position of the electric switches for the gadgets in the kitchen.

He reviewed books and corrected proofs. He had his desk at the *New Yorker*, where he worked regular hours and beyond. William Shawn, editor of the *New Yorker*, admired his writing and provided continuous secretarial help in relays. Books were read out to him, as also galley proofs, word by word including punctuation marks; he dictated corrections and checked them in subsequent proofs. He not only wrote stories and sketches but also on technical subjects. Once he was away for a couple of weeks to study a desalination plant somewhere, and then wrote a detailed report as a *New Yorker* feature.

In his company one forgot the fact, or rather failed to notice, that he could not see. He had developed compensatory faculties, which enabled him to perceive, understand and implant in memory, every detail of his surroundings.

One evening he had tickets for a play and invited me to join him. When we came out of the theatre, he analysed and discussed the play all through the evening. He attended parties and recognized everyone by voice, also entertained at home, selecting and mixing drinks for his guests from a cocktail cabinet.

When we last met, he lived uptown on Fifth Avenue, eleventh floor of an apartment. When he started out he carefully locked the door, never misplaced the key, walked down the passage to the elevator, crossed the hallway, summoned a taxi, reached his office on the eighteenth floor of a building on West 25th Street, all by himself without the slightest error at any point of his passage, even on a bleak day when a freak weather in April had left a seven-foot pile of snow in New York streets. A marvel, whom I cannot forget, though I have lost touch with him.

1992

CROWDED DAY

SOME YEARS AGO I ATTENDED THE OPENING ceremony of the Air-India terminal at the Kennedy airport in New York. The Air-India PRO was keen that I should attend it. Thirty limousines were engaged to transport the guests to the terminal from the Air-India office on Park Avenue. We would take off at ten and return to the starting point after lunch. I pleaded, 'But I'm a vegetarian.' 'Don't worry, many of our guests are also vegetarians. But if you were not strict, you could enjoy it. J.R.D. is bringing special items—tandoori chicken, etc. Most of our guests are looking forward to the special luncheon. You don't have to worry, we'll take care of you.'

J.R.D. Tata was there, and after his speech he proceeded to cut the ribbon—when a terrific squeal startled the distinguished assembly, for the scissors he held slightly nicked the finger of a charming air-hostess who held the ribbon. J.R.D. said, 'Terribly sorry. With a pretty face before me I could not help it.'

After this unusual inauguration we trooped up-stairs to the assembly hall. Waiters bearing trays of titbits and drinks were going round. Not knowing what was what, I let the trays pass, and stood aside with folded arms. My PRO friend sidled up to whisper: 'We are proposing a toast . . . . Take a glass and raise it with others . . . .' I picked up a bowl with 'beaded bubbles winking at the brim', resembling Spencer's soda water of other days. The PRO whispered: 'It's only champagne, absolutely safe.' I sipped when others sipped. It tasted slightly sour. I circulated around with the glass in hand, touching its rim with my lips now and then. Whenever its level went down, the eagle-eyed waiters refilled it. I didn't keep count, but spent over an hour chit-chatting, nodding and smiling at all and sundry.

Buffet lunch was ready at another section of the hall. I saw nothing I could accept among the delicacies spread out. J.R.D. Tata had not brought anything for me. It was two o'clock when I realized that there was going to be no lunch for me. I spotted the PRO far off in a group, busy helping some guests. I went up and asked, 'Where do I find the vegetarian stuff?'

'Oh yes, let me find out . . . .' He returned after investigation, 'Some sandwiches, over there—I'll get you some.' When he brought me a plate of sandwiches, I took a bite and realized that it was something soft and rubbery and mustard-tasting. I asked a waiter, 'What sandwich is this?' 'Maybe ox-tongue, sir . . . .'

I hurried down and out to find a spot to spit it out, and then saw no reason to stay on; but found transport to take me back to Manhattan. It was nearing three. I realized that it was time for my next appointment, at the United Nations. A friend had secured me a pass to watch a debate on Kashmir between M.C. Chagla and Zulfikar Ali Bhutto. The hall was packed but I found a comfortable seat and felt drowsy; rousing myself with an effort I wanted to get up and shout, 'Less noise please; you bore me.'

Bhutto's retinue was large and I wanted to ask, 'Mr Bhutto, is it necessary to have an army of file-bearers? Chagla is managing with less.' I found it difficult to follow the proceedings. With the earphone on and fiddling with different buttons at my elbow, I amused myself for a while listening to the simultaneous translations of the speeches in French, German, Spanish and so on. In no language did it make sense. Officious men were hurrying up and down carrying papers to their bosses seated in the front row. I was not impressed, 'This is all a show. All actors, "comedians" as Graham Greene called them. No more of this.' I got up abruptly and made my exit. I was hungry. I went in search of T.J. Natarajan, who was my friend, philosopher and guide in New York. He was in his office. He suggested, 'Why don't you go to the Meditation Room while I finish some work?' The Meditation Room, a little soundproof chamber with a few chairs placed facing an abstract granite sculpture under a ray of light, used to be my retreat whenever I happened to visit the UN building, but now I was in no mood to meditate. I explained my predicament to my friend. 'Let us go home,' he said at once.

We took the train for Roosevelt Avenue and reached his home. I managed somehow to travel all that distance and then walk from the station to his house. He understood what was wrong with me and said, 'These parties are not for people like us.'

After dinner I felt normal, well enough go back to Hotel Chelsea on West 23rd Street. I woke up at ten next morning and realized that I had slept with my shoes on. The day ahead was crowded with engagements. I took off the shoes and moved towards the kitchen to make coffee. When I walked, I realized that my legs did not belong to me and the directions were slightly confusing. Still I resolved to go through the day's schedule.

My first engagement was at the Time-Life office, for a conference with the *Life International* editor, Cal Whipple, who had commissioned me to write a piece on Mahatma Gandhi. We were meeting in order to discuss and settle its final shape. Four more editors arrived and sat around. The discussion started. 'What we are proposing is a comparison with Nehru, whose social philosophy is so different from Gandhi's. Do you think it's possible? You will have to rewrite the Gandhi piece which we have in hand .... Gandhi believed in the spinning wheel, while Nehru said factory chimneys were his temples ....'

'Yes, yes, of course,' I said mechanically. I found it irksome to be sitting up and talking. Suddenly I asked, 'Cal, would you mind if I lie down on the couch over there, while you gentlemen discuss the details?' They were taken aback, but Cal said, 'Certainly ....' I moved over to a couch and stretched myself comfortably, and listened to their talk pretending to participate in the discussion from my recumbent position. The discussion, however, fizzled out. Others left, Cal alone remained in his chair and asked, 'R.K., what's the matter? Are you not feeling well?'

'My head is OK, but since this morning, I find my legs acting in a funny manner.'

'What have you been up to?'

I explained, and added, 'I took just a little champagne.'

'How little?'

'I can't say, they kept refilling the glass.'

'Oh, I understand now, it is a hangover in simple language. Go back to your room and sleep it off. We will meet again.'

I went down and sat on the bench in the Plaza where a fountain was playing. I took stock of myself. That day was important. I had a series of engagements. My first task would be to reach the Pathe

Theatre for a preview of *The Guide* in English. Pearl Buck was coming all the way from Connecticut, Tad Danielweki who directed the film would be there, and also some film critics. The preview was in order to trim up the film before showing it to the exhibitors.

I sat there on the bench wondering how to reach the theatre. My great inclination was to flop down anywhere and sleep it off as Cal Whipple had suggested. My legs seemed to function now but were not very steady yet. Foolish of me to have yielded to that invitation. My immediate resolve was never to accept any invitation for any opening ceremony or closing ceremony anywhere on earth, and never to accept even a glass of water from anyone. People were likely to drug me.

Champagne which appeared innocent like distilled water was but a time-bomb. One would be safer probably with known plebian drinks, which made one tipsy right at the start, but this was a dangerous drink with its delayed action. I was reduced to this foolish state and wasted everyone's time, neutralizing a conference on Gandhi and Nehru while lying inanely on a couch.

I asked myself, 'Am I a Man or Mouse? If I am the former I must possess a mind which should take control immediately. I need only the will-power to get up and walk.' I got up determined to remain firm on foot. Should I move to my right or left? If I turned right I could reach my hotel, go up the elevator and seek comforting oblivion in bed. If I turned left I could reach Pathe Theatre.

I took out of my pocket Tad's letter and checked the address. 'Walk down the avenue and turn right and left again, and go on and on till you see the "Pathe" signboard.' I had no idea how far to go, but I started out determinedly, Robert Frost's lines echoing in my head, 'Miles to go . . . .' I was determined not to give in to negative thoughts, and tried to erase from memory yesterday's lapses. I walked past several 'Walk' and 'Don't Walk' signs. Now I felt 80 per cent normal and presently a 100 per cent when a sudden cloud-burst drenched me to the skin.

When I entered the preview theatre I was feeling fresh and buoyant. Pearl Buck and the rest were astonished to see me enter like the Rain God. The screening started immediately. Dev Anand and Waheeda Rehman were uttering sentiments and sentences for which I was not responsible. I accepted this *Guide* as a bastard offspring of my novel. Being in a forgiving mood and cool-headed, I let it pass without a fight. I knew that the picture was just glossy nonsense. What if ? Without argument or controversy, I quietly slipped away, while Pearl Buck and others were discussing strategies for winning the Oscar or Grand Prix at some film festival with their version of *The Guide.*

My next halt was at the Indian consulate where M.F. Husain was exhibiting his latest paintings among which a portrait of myself was included. I had given him a sitting the previous week, but when I saw the portrait, I had remarked that I didn't look like myself. He had smiled at my lack of taste and replied that I wouldn't know my real self. I left it at that and adjourned to a room for recording an interview for a radio broadcast.

After the usual questions, which I could answer while asleep, the interviewer asked, 'Are you pleased with the film version of your *Guide*?'

'No,' I answered clearly, 'but anyhow they were good enough to retain the title of my story, the rest is their very own . . . .'

1992

KOREAN GRASS

'LAST EVENING I VISITED A FRIEND AND found his lawn extremely green and flourishing,' said the Minister to his secretary, 'you go there and get all the information you can about it.'

The secretary brought the information, 'It's called Korean Grass, sir. It grows easily and needs no mowing.'

'I like the idea. So much economy in labour and machinery, if it needs no lawnmower! All that energy and equipment could be diverted to national development. Investigate further and find out how our cattle react to Korean Grass. Either way it'll be a blessing. If cows eat Korean Grass, my visit to Korea will prove a blessing to our National Dairy Development. If our cows won't accept this wonder grass, even that will be a blessing in disguise; then our gardens will automatically be protected from the cattle menace, even without gates and compound walls for our buildings—like other civilized countries where residential buildings are divided only by lawns and pathways and no gates at all.

'All that material and hardware could be saved for a better purpose. We shall be compelled to develop new architectural values and outlook with the advent of Korean Grass. Get all the data on the Korean stuff immediately, I must prepare a statement on the subject. Telephone the Director of Agriculture and also the Director-General of Animal Husbandry who will have expert knowledge about the habits and preferences of cows. This Korean question has several aspects; we must not overlook any aspect. When we are assured our cows will eat this grass we must organize a National Convention with the motto, "K.G. will save our Nation, with limitless pasture, providing milk for the millions."

'TV and radio must allot prime time for promoting this proposal. I will study at first-hand the technique and extent of cultivation of Korean Grass in Korea.'

'There are two Koreas, sir, North and South.'

'I will have to visit both—I have long wanted to visit North Korea—I hear that Hanoi is charming.'

'Hanoi is North Vietnam, sir . . . .'

'That makes no difference. I will visit both Koreas and then Vietnam.'

'I also found in some houses Mexican Grass, which is soft and green.'

'Mexico also must be included. It must be a round-the-world trip. I want to cover all the grass-growing countries on this trip so that we may plan total greenery in this part of the globe. Grass is not only fodder but also indispensable for golf, tennis and cricket. We will be on top in future Olympics if we provide proper playgrounds for our athletes and sportsmen.'

'Perhaps, if I may humbly suggest, we may hold an International Grass Convention in Delhi, sir.'

'Later, of course, as of now draw up a tour programme immediately.'

'Will it be a delegation, sir?'

'Depends on the budget . . . . I must discuss it with the Finance Ministry. I want to start on this project at once, and see it through before Parliament meets. There are rumours that the Opposition is planning a no-confidence motion. If it is true, one cannot foresee what will happen. Take care that you don't mention it to the press, which will certainly distort our aims and create an uproar in Parliament when it meets.'

'Your Honour may depend on me to work it out on a confidential and emergency basis.'

'That is right.'

'Sir, what about the staff accompanying Your Honour?'

'That is all a matter of detail which we will examine in due course. First draw up a tour programme, and book a round-the-world ticket, First Class.'

'Which airline, sir?'

'I will prefer any foreign line though according to government rules it must be Air-India. Remember that my daughter and son-in-law will have to come with me; after my last operation, I am not allowed to travel alone. This important point should be emphasized while drafting the proposal, when it goes to the Prime Minister. I am sure he will feel happy to find me actively doing something as he has kept me on without being able to allot any portfolio to me so far. He will probably name me Minister for Greenery.'

'The title, sir, reminds me of a film I saw long ago which was called *How Green was my Valley*.'

'Excellent, who wrote it?'

'Must be Shakespeare. All good quotations were written by Shakespeare, sir.'

'Undoubtedly. Also find out if he has any humorous anecdotes we may find relevant.'

1992

MINISTER WITHOUT PORTFOLIO

THE MINISTER WAS DEJECTED WHEN HE STRODE in, but he assumed a jaunty air to impress his secretary, who already possessed full knowledge, through the telephone, of what had transpired at the Prime Minister's office. The least-noticed, self-effacing factotum in that office was the informant, and he had kept up a running commentary of their meeting.

'The Hon'ble Prime Minister is receiving the Hon'ble Minister and they are both seated on a sofa conversing in a low tone. But my ears are sharp while I wait at the door to be summoned. After the courtesies the PM said, "I have gone through your proposal to visit Korea for its grass. But Korean grass is available for the asking anywhere; you don't have to go so far to study its cultivation, there is nothing to learn. It is the simplest thing to grow. Don't you notice that my compound is overrun with it? Everywhere it is grown."

'"Yes, sir, I know it, but I thought that if there is any special technique they are holding back . . . ." The Prime Minister did not let him complete the sentence but rang the bell for tea. As I was bringing in the tray I could hear him say, "Concentrate on problems of your constituency, spend more time there, even locking up your residence in Delhi. Strengthen our party there—that's our need of the hour." After tea he rang the bell for the next visitor,' concluded the factotum.

Now, after coming back to his office, the Minister tried to look cheerful and told his secretary, 'The Prime Minister thinks we should have early rains this year, otherwise we will face problems. He wants me to be watchful and strengthen our party, and also concentrate on national integration on an emergency basis.'

'His opinion of the Korean grass, sir?'

'Oh, we had more urgent matters to discuss . . . . Reading his mind, I think he has some other plans for me.'

'Maybe, sir, a Governorship . . . four posts are falling vacant next year.'

'Hm, maybe, but don't even whisper about it beyond the four walls of this room . . . . Personally, I would not care for it, but if I am commanded in the interests of the country to accept it, as a soldier I will obey the PM as he knows best what is good for the country.'

A few days later, a news item caught the Minister's attention. The report said, 'At Bannerghatta open zoo in Bangalore, a little girl who had gone to watch the animals was mauled by a tiger.'

'Horrible, find out how it happened. You must get me a first-hand report immediately.'

'Yes, sir, I will deal with it on an emergency basis.' He was ready with the report in a couple of hours: 'Sir, I called up the editor of a daily in Bangalore to verify the news. I told the editor, "The Hon'ble Minister demands immediate, full information on this news item." But he said it is all an exaggeration by the media to embarrass the Chief Minister. He assures me, sir, that there was no such incident. If Your Honour will permit, I will go to Bangalore and find out the truth and bring an authentic report within twenty-four hours, sir.'

'Let me think it over . . . .' The Minister thought it over and decided, 'I had better go to Bangalore myself, inspect the tiger and return the same day. Find out if an Indian Air Force plane will be available to fly to Bangalore airport, and a helicopter from the airport to Bannerghatta, which opportunity I can also utilize to survey the flood-stricken areas and assess the relief measures needed.'

His dreams extended to a visit to Africa at a later date to study the precautions taken at safaris in Kenya, 'Where, I am sure, vehicles in which visitors are taken through the lion country are specially designed and of steel of the finest temper. I hope you realize that in a safari the visitors are caged while the wild animals are free. They must have some special technique for such things, otherwise so many casualties are likely to befall the tourists who flock there. We must learn to protect our children and adults from tigers. It's the government's duty to ensure safety in our zoos. Tomorrow, the first thing, you must call the Director-General of Animals-In-Captivity. I want you to talk to him.'

The next day the secretary reported, 'I went through the Civil Service list; there is no such post in our government, sir.'

'Scandalous! They must create one soon if they care for our national welfare . . . . Make a note of it, I'll speak to the PM some time. Meanwhile, draw up a tour programme for my south Indian visit. An IAF plane must be requisitioned.'

'Sir, if I may draw Your Honour's attention, such a requisition must go through the PM's office.'

'Oh God, again the PM's office!' cried the Minister, but the secretary looked away and pretended not to have heard it. When he did finally prepare the tour programme, he was told, 'No IAF plane can be spared as the situation in the border areas does not warrant diversion of the Air Force for anything other than defence purposes. Also the object of the Minister's proposed visit is not clear. If he wants to survey the flood areas, he must understand that the floods in both Kaveri and Kabini have subsided. The State authorities have provided appropriate relief measures. Moreover the only helicopter, the Chief Minister's, will not be available since it has been dismantled for repairs. The Chief Minister himself has not been able to visit some of the problem areas as planned. The whole report of the incident of the tiger is controversial and tendentious. In any case, the centre cannot take cognizance of tiger attacks. Even if they are true, the matter is solely a State subject.'

1993

THE JUDGE

THE TALKATIVE MAN SAID (TO HIS USUAL evening audience lounging on the pedestal of Lawley Statue):

It was an unwise decision on my part to have accepted the judgeship. I was forced into it by my well-wishers. God save us from our well-wishers and relatives. Far too many of them all around. I sometimes wish that I had been born in isolation in some desert. Here Malgudi was swarming with kinsmen. Every street housed a cousin, a round-about nephew or a remote uncle, so that unless I dashed past a door, I had no chance of reaching my destination in time. "Hai! Don't go, I must tell you something," one or the other would cry at the sight of me.

Baited by such an invitation, I would stop and listen to family gossip, discussion of national events and disasters, and when the speaker paused for breath, pick up my bicycle and be on my way again. I was a news reporter in those days, wandering all over the town, ending up at The Boardless to recoup my energy with coffee and snacks. Quite an active, happy life. Sheltered securely in our ancestral home in Kabir Street, I was a contented man.

This perfect life threatened to come to an end once. While passing Grove Street one morning, an uncle of mine hailed me from his door—that horrible man spent his hours watching the street. He said to me, "Now listen to this attentively. Did you see in the morning paper an announcement calling young men with a law degree or journalistic experience to apply for a special judge's post—a new policy in order to clear the arrears in law courts? Why don't you present yourself for the interview at Madras? They will pay your rail-fare."

I could not picture myself as a judge, sitting high, making pronouncements. The picture was too absurd. I suffered from severe short-sight, minus twelve being the strength of my glasses which weighed down my nose and misshaped it. Without my glasses, I could not distinguish a mud wall from my mother-in-law, if I had one. So I said, "With such thick glasses one can't occupy a judge's seat." But my uncle brushed aside my objection, "Thick glasses add dignity to a man in high position." I was weak-minded enough to accept his advice. Not content with advising, he spread the news far and wide, and very soon. I was overwhelmed with congratulations.

I had not suspected that there could be so many in this world anxious to see me elevated to a judge's seat. I was getting tired of the advice I was receiving at every turn, "The important thing is the interview. Being a journalist you will get through creditably. We will arrange a grand celebration if you are selected. Do your best." Even our Varma, the level-headed proprietor of The Boardless looked on me with awe, and murmured in an undertone, while I sat at his side sipping coffee: "The important thing is the interview. You must do your best."

Eventually, I appeared before an august body assembled in a Chamber at the Madras High Court. Five men, two on each side of a chairman, gems culled from five corners of our country, were seated on a platform, while I was given a wooden-stool to face them. They put me at my ease with some personal questions such as "Are you married or single?" "What is your weight?" "Do you like wheat or rice?" Then they put to me questions to plumb my general knowledge, intelligence, and judgement, such as "What is the average rainfall in North-East Somalia?" "Name a tenth-century ruler of Outer Mongolia?" "Define in not more than four sentences the 'Loch Ness monster'." Finally, they asked why I wanted to be a judge and how I would handle a murder trial. I promptly said, "I would hang the murderer without any delay."

The last-mentioned question turned out to be prophetic, as I found myself, in course of time, sitting over a baffling murder case. Day after day, the case dragged on. I did my best to avoid a decision by postponement on flimsy excuses. "At the alleged time of the crime, Your Honour, A-3 was at a post office."

"Which post office?"

"I'll find out, Your Honour."

"Look sharp. It is a crucial point. Till you are able to name the post office and file the report, hearing is adjourned."

And the court rose for the day, the seven poor souls in chains were marched off, and the lawyer and the public prosecutor turned their attention to other miscreants in another court, while I grandly strode back to my Chamber, shut the door, and stretched myself on a sofa and fell asleep.

I really had no idea how long I could go on postponing a decision. It was a complicated case. Some months before, on the highway between Kumbam and Malgudi, a man travelling in a bus was dragged out and hacked to death. The bus was full in addition to a conductor and the driver, but none saw it happen. The driver just said, "A blue Ambassador car blocked the road, and when I applied the brake, four men rushed into the bus, dragged away a passenger seated in the last row. I don't know what happened afterwards."

"Why could you not see what happened?"

"The four men who entered the bus threw chilli powder in our eyes and dragged the man out."

"How many were seated in the bus?"

"About forty, Your Honour."

"How much chilli powder would be needed to blind forty pairs of eyes, and how many hands would be required to sprinkle the said powder simultaneously into all those forty pairs of eyes, not to mention the driver and the conductor, and how much powder was swept up from the floor of the bus after the event?"

This sounded to me an extremely subtle point from the defence lawyer. I noted it down ceremoniously. I was getting engrossed in the story and wished that I could be left alone to enjoy it without judging its merits. I asked now, "Did the police make any arrangement to collect the chilli powder from the bus, and if so, let the exhibit be marked, numbered and filed."

Thereby, I gained another term of irresolution. When the case came up again, the defending lawyer created a fresh problem. He objected to the post-mortem report as being unconvincing. The description of the injuries on the deceased looked more like tooth-and-claw marks than those inflicted by blunt or sharp instruments; the wounds must have been inflicted by a tiger which was reported to be sighted off and on in that area, attacking cattle and men.

"Can you produce a certified report of the tiger's havoc?"

"Yes, Your Honour. I have the ranger's certificate, but it must be countersigned by the Conservator of Forests who is away in Africa for a wildlife conference."

"When is he expected to return?"

"I will have to find out, Your Honour."

The prosecutor opposed this excuse for postponement as being vague, but I overruled his objection and posted the case for the fifteenth of the following month. The prosecution utilized the time to garnish and polish their story further so that they might present a convincing picture next time.

The deceased and the accused were rival applicants for a licence to sell arrack at a certain tavern. The deceased had his rival beaten up three days before the alleged incident and also threatened to molest his wife. The police had also registered a case against him at about that time. I made note of it but suddenly reverted to the tiger which I thought was more interesting than the police. "We will revert to the question of the arrack licence later. But, I must know now if pugmarks of the tiger were found at the scene of the crime?"

"Yes, Your Honour."

"Were they measured and photographed?"

"They could be measured only partially, Your Honour, because a herd of buffaloes was reported to have crossed the same track later; in spite of it, we did obtain certain photographs and measurements."

"Of the buffalo hoofs?" I could not resist asking, which provoked laughter in the Court. Encouraged by it, I added, "Possibly, the deceased came to a sorry end through getting mixed up among the stampeding buffaloes." More laughter.

"Possibly, Your Honour, but, it was also not

unlikely that he was mauled by a tiger stalking the buffalo herd. He must have been knocked down senseless with a swing of its powerful paw as is the habit with such beasts."

"Why did it not eat him off? The post–mortem report makes no mention of any chewed-off bits from the body. No portion is missing?"

"Because at that very moment, a village procession passed with tom-toms and flares and the tiger must have run away," said the defence lawyer.

"Can you get a sworn statement from the village munsif about the procession?" the prosecutor interrupted.

"Your Honour, I submit that this court's valuable time is being sidetracked to listen to cock-and-bull stories."

"Rather buffalo and tiger story," I said, and there was laughter in the court. I was pleased with the way I was amusing them. Such entertainment could not last forever. I had to decide soon. Looking at the seven men before me accused of murder, I felt that if I sentenced to death any or all of them, I could be considered an eighth murderer. They had, at least, the excuse of rivalry, revenge or resentment, while I would be only a coldblooded hangman's partner, nothing less, if I pronounced a death sentence. I was obsessed with the feeling (like Roger de Coverley of

Addison's Essays), that much might be said on both sides.

When the defence lawyer argued, I nearly wept for the poor fellows arrayed before me. When the prosecutor dilated upon the nefariousness of the conspirators, I felt that without the formality of a trial they should be lined up and shot. One helpless man to be chased and butchered by seven with crowbars and hatchets and cycle chains while he was running for his dear life. Oh! the thought was too horrible to contemplate. They were *rakshasas.*

When inspired thus I seized my pen and drafted in a frenzy a model death sentence for most of them, except two youths who had only strayed into evil company. Those two boys looked tender and seemed incapable of any violence. But the prosecution had included them in a package—those boys being energetic, were said to have raced along, overtaken their victim and suddenly turning round, tripped him up, and held him down while the seniors dismembered him.

But, in cross-examination they denied everything. The pair was from different villages, one working in a cycle-repair shop and the other a rag-picker, collecting scraps for a waste-paper merchant. While passing that way, each on his own business, they had stopped on seeing the dead body. When the police arrived, they were both bundled into the van and detained in a police lock-up till they put their thumb impressions on some papers put before them.

The prosecutor cross-examined till the boys messed up their own earlier versions, and entangled themselves in contradictions. Whatever it might be, I decided to give the young fellows the benefit of doubt. At this point, I received a warning from the Chief Justice not to prolong the case, in keeping with the government's new policy of abolishing law's delays. I had to submit immediately a report of my hearings and the adjournments up-to-date, whereupon the Chief Justice set a time limit for me to conclude and deliver judgement, giving me fifteen days from 5 to 20 June—on 21 June I must announce who was to hang.

I felt desperate. When I glanced out of the window I envied people who went about their business without a care, not having to judge a murder. I cursed the day I accepted this profession and I cursed that busy body—my uncle of Grove Street—who had pushed me into it. I told myself devoutly, "Only God can help me."

Our family deity watched us from the temple on Tirupati Hills; thither I went carrying a suitcase full of documents. I stood praying in the sanctum (being a judge I was ushered into the presence of God through a special door though others had to wait in a long queue outside). The image of Lord Venkateswara, decorated with flowers and gold and gems, scintillated in the flickering oil lamps and camphor flame. I prostrated before the image and prayed, "Save me from making a fool of myself. From my analysis of the evidence, I feel accused one and three are to be hanged and numbers two, four, and five to be sentenced for life—for abetment and conspiracy. A-6 and 7—two years' rigorous imprisonment, more as a corrective, being only youth found in bad company.

"I have not put pen to paper yet, waiting for a sign from the Almighty. I will sit down here for a moment and begin the first few lines in your divine presence, work on it all night in my room and pronounce judgement on 21 June as ordered by the Chief. Please guide me, my Lord."

At this moment, I became aware of a slight pressure on my shoulder, followed by a blankness before my eyes. Everything vanished in a profound haze. The image of God which was scintillating a few moments ago was no longer visible. A devotee waiting outside cried, "Sir, there goes a monkey with your spectacles." Another man said, "Now it has gone out and is going up the outer tower." "If you throw a banana at him, he will catch the fruit and let go your glasses," said another.

Someone else suggested, "There must be a monkey-trainer somewhere who can call it back if you give him five rupees."

I remembered the warning notices pasted on the temple pillars "Beware of Monkeys!" "Guard your spectacles and handbags!" Generations of monkeys flourished in the spacious temple at various corners, perched on pillars and roofs and were in the habit of darting down and snatching away fruits from the hands of pilgrims and also spectacles and other detachable articles on any person.

I was helped to get back home in the town. It took a couple of days to get a new pair of glasses compounded. Till then, I had to live the life of a blind man as an atonement for the sin of accepting a judgeship without possessing a decisive mind. I called my steno and dictated my judgement (when I got a new pair of glasses)—a verdict of not guilty—and ordered the immediate release of all the seven accused. I viewed the monkey as a bearer of a divine message in response to my prayer.

*

At this point, one of his listeners questioned the Talkative Man, 'We have been meeting you every day; when were you a judge and where?'

'You demand an explanation, do you? You won't get it. I will only quote my friend Falstaff in Shakespeare's play. He was asked to explain how or why of certain episodes. His reply was, "No . . . if reasons were as plenty as blackberries I would give no man a reason upon compulsion." '

1993

VISITOR

THE MINISTER BELIEVED IN CONSUMING A sumptuous breakfast. After a proper breakfast, one's mind, body and soul attained perfect harmony, and one was ready to tackle any problem, national, international or personal. Fortunately his wife preferred to stay back at the constituency in their ancient home, leaving him free to dictate his wants to the cook without inhibition. She was an interfering sort, a watchdog of the cholesterol level in his system. Women never understood that it was unnatural to starve and a little bulge around the waist did no one any harm, and in no way interfered with one's functioning as a minister.

'Sound mind in a sound body' was a piece of unassailable logic, unattainable without a planned breakfast. All other meals were, no doubt, important but secondary. He did not want to lose his concentration while eating, hence never invited anyone to join him at breakfast. Most people were envious and dyspeptic, unable to digest even arrowroot gruel, and cast an evil eye on one who enjoyed his food.

Half an hour before arriving at the breakfast table he ordered a glass of orange juice with a dash of salt and pepper. When he felt sure that it had gone down well and was out of the way, he started with four idlis and two vadas submerged in sambar. Whatever reservations one might have about south Indians (especially in regard to their mulish antipathy to Hindi), one must feel eternally grateful to them for composing this gastronomic symphony for breakfast.

Idli was followed by golden-hued aloo paratha, two pieces of shredded wheat (imported) with honey and milk, and then cereals with nut raisins, a one-egg fluffy omelette spiced with onion and capsicum, a crescent of papaya, Kabul grapes, sapota, etc., all washed down with a mug of sweet tea. After this performance, he entered the hall chewing paan, ready to face the day's tasks and problems and settled in his sofa.

Into this tranquil state crashed his PA announcing a visitor. 'Who is he? Has he an appointment? All right, send him in. My duty is to receive complaints. Has he any? It is my duty to listen to people's grievances, and tackle any problem affecting public welfare.'

The visitor was seated in an armless wooden chair placed close to the Minister's sofa. The man looked sulky and held out a thick wad of typewritten material for the Minister's acceptance.

'What is it?' asked the Minister.

'Read it, and you will know,' said the other.

'Are you commanding me?' asked the Minister, and sounded the buzzer for his PA and said, 'Receive that memorandum and see what it is.' Clutching it firmly the visitor said, 'We didn't prepare it for your PA. We demand your attention. If you look at my card you will know that: I am President of . . . . ' He turned to the PA and ordered him to fetch his visiting-card. While the PA was gone to get the card, he talked on and on non-stop, much of it incomprehensible to the Minister, and tried once again to thrust his memorandum on the Minister. 'Read it and you will understand our problem,' he said.

'What problem?'

'It is all in that, read it . . . . '

'It is too bulky,' wailed the Minister. 'You expect me to go through it?'

'Yes, line by line, why not?'

'I have better business.'

'What better business? You are here to serve the people who have put you in your present position through votes and maintain you through taxes.'

'I am busy. Tell me briefly what you want.'

The man snatched the volume from a little teapoy on which he had rested it, and walked out muttering something. The Minister watched his exit helplessly, turned to his PA and asked, 'Did he say anything while leaving . . . some word sounding like fool?'

'If you will excuse me I heard it as "bloody fool", sir.'

'How dare he? Call him back . . . . We can't let him get away with it.'

'We must have an excuse to call him in again, sir.'

'Run up and say I want to offer him tea . . . . ' He called his cook and ordered tea. The visitor returned and accepted the tea.

After the tea ceremony the Minister asked, 'Did you say "fool"?'

'No. I just said "foolish".'

'Why, have you any reason?'

'I can give you forty-eight reasons.'

'Oh! Give it in writing. Otherwise I can't take note of it.'

'It will make a second volume. All right, I will send it by registered post,' he said and rose abruptly and left.

The Minister watched his exit helplessly again, and swore, 'He must be dismissed immediately.'

'We can't dismiss him, he is not in government service, sir . . . . '

'Then what shall we do?'

'We must appoint him first and then dismiss . . . .'

'Good idea, but how?'

'We have his visiting-card, sir, calls himself president of something. Your honour has powers to nationalize it, and appoint him as president, and then dismiss him.'

'Excellent plan. Draft a nationalization order and send it for publication in the *Gazette*, get the compiler on the phone, I will speak to him . . . . '

'Yes, sir.'

1993

SAMPATH'S ELEPHANT

LYLE BLAIR, THE DIRECTOR OF MICHIGAN STATE University Press at East Lansing, an Australian who loved my writing and while in London published my *Bachelor of Arts* in Pocket Books, took upon himself the task of publishing my novels in the United States, where I was unknown. He brought out all my novels in impressive hard-cover editions in order to introduce me to American readers. The last title he brought out was *Mr. Sampath (Printer of Malgudi)*.

At Algonquin the occasion was celebrated through an elaborate cocktail party to which many critics and publishers in New York were invited. (I have described the event in *My Dateless Diary*.)

Lyle Blair was first and foremost a Malgudi enthusiast, (I avoid the word fan, which I dislike) so much so that he routed his passage through Mysore once on his way to Sydney from Michigan. I had him as a guest at the Mysore Sports Club, and he was charmed by his surroundings, with a tree-covered boulevard in front and Chamundi Hill looking over the landscape ahead of the club veranda, and light country traffic on the road, caravans of bullock carts, groups of villagers returning home behind the Lalitha Mahal Palace where the boulevard terminated.

I took him round in my Morris Minor; he was, thank God, not interested in shopping, souvenirs or novelties, but loved to watch the streets and bazaars and market-place and was trying to piece together like a jig-saw puzzle components of Malgudi as he had visualized it. But his main mission seemed to be to meet 'Sampath', the original of the Printer of Malgudi. The greatest event for him was to visit Sampath at his little press known to the world as City Power Press, which was no more than a single-room front office where Sampath sat at his desk with four chairs for visitors and a treadle with a single typesetting board in the background, all out of public view.

Sampath overwhelmed the visitor with his courtly welcome; Lyle began to feel that my picture of him in the novel did not bring out his real dimension. Coffee and snacks were brought in by his children, nephews and nieces in the large family: they were so perfectly drilled for the task that they glided in one after another like fairies bearing in their arms trays of heavenly sweets and bowls of nectar. When they left Sampath asked, 'Mr Blair, is there anything else you would like?'

Lyle thought it over and said, 'I'd like to see an elephant.' Sampath said, 'All right, I'll see if I can manage it,' and went up to the threshold and watched the street ahead and suddenly clapped his hands and shouted, 'Hey, come here . . . .' And lo! there came an elephant with a mahout perched on it. It was a coincidence in a million, an elephant passing-show materializing at the wave of a hand.

Sampath however did not make much of it, expressed no surprise, as if it were a normal occurrence at the City Power Press. He was a consummate actor; the 'Power Press' turned out printed matter only when he was off-stage or not rehearsing Moliere's plays in some college society, training young men for a show from time to time. It was often his old foreman who had to answer customers demanding a promised proof. I myself tried to produce a quarterly magazine in his press and ultimately gave up after a few issues, in order not to jeopardize our friendship. (I have explained it all in *My Days.*)

Now to return to the elephant. Sampath let Lyle touch the elephant and go round it and told him to address a few encouraging words to the mahout and translated it. Lyle offered money to the mahout, but Sampath held his hand back, 'No, no . . . as it is on the house,' and telling the mahout to come and see him later, he dismissed the elephant with a flourish of his hand. Lyle never got over this surprise and later in Michigan he kept repeating to every person known to him, 'Do you know Narayan's friend Sampath is a real conjuror? He could produce an elephant by a wave of his fingers!'

On the whole, Lyle's visit was a magical one for him, as he said before he left for Sydney next morning. Before leaving, he said, 'Will you be willing to go to the Philippines to write on the life of President Magsaysay who died in an air crash? I can arrange it if you are willing to accept this assignment.'

1993

IN THE PHILIPPINES

One September evening I landed in Manila from Hong Kong, with no idea of what I was going to do, with no notion whatever about Magsaysay. At the airport they detained me, offering a chair in a corner of the hall. After all the passengers had left, the officer beckoned me to approach him. He studied my passport page by page, comparing the photo with the person standing before him and then asked, 'Why have you come here?'

'To write on . . .' I said, and explained my mission. At the mention of Magsaysay, he relaxed his grimness. He was in khaki uniform with colour strips on his chest. It looked as if he had the authority to knock down or imprison anyone entering his country. 'Is anyone coming to meet you?' 'I don't know.' 'Go up and look if anyone has come to receive you.' I walked up to a wall he indicated, which was perforated. I peered through the circular holes in the wall and saw in the darkness shadowy figures outside, all Filipinos, naturally.

I pretended to look for someone and returned to the officer, 'No, no one has come.'

'What will be your address in Manila?' I blinked, not being prepared for so much cross-examination. He became more and more suspicious, and treated me as a spy or an illegal immigrant. The hall was deserted, all the passengers who had arrived with me had been cleared. I asked him in a fit of desperation, 'Why are you holding me up like this?' He did not reply. 'I should like to reach my hotel. I've travelled a long way,' I mumbled.

'Which hotel?'

'I'll find one.'

'Any idea where?'

'Look here,' I said finally, 'I have come to write a book on your late President Magsaysay . . . .' The mention of Magsaysay, again, at once changed the atmosphere; he became solicitous and called up someone and ordered him to book a hotel and a taxi for me. 'You are a Narayan? Any relation of Jayaprakash Narayan?'

'In a way, all Narayans are of one family . . .' I said casually.

*

I was in the dining-hall of the hotel—an attendant came to say, 'An inspector from the health bureau is waiting in your room, sir—' I hurried up to my room on the first floor. An officer had made himself comfortable in a chair by my bed. He said, 'I didn't want to wait in the lounge.' I did not want to question him. He wanted my passport and air ticket. He asked, 'You have passed through Calcutta? Your health certificate, please.' He looked at it and said, 'You had cholera inoculation. That's good. Still, you will please present yourself at the Bureau of Health at ten tomorrow morning.'

'Why?'

'You have passed through Calcutta—Bengal is a cholera zone. We may have to quarantine you—'

I protested and explained that I had only been at the Dum Dum airport.

He ignored my explanation and asked, 'Have you brought any foodstuff?'

'No,' I said brazenly, hoping he would not turn round and notice three Horlicks bottles filled with spicy mixtures and pastes to be mixed with plain rice, which my sister had insisted upon my taking with me. He was, for all his grimness, an inefficient fellow, who did not have the sense to turn round and notice the Horlicks bottles, though he menaced me, 'If you have brought any foodstuff we'll have to confiscate and destroy it. If you make a false statement, it will be serious.' After he left I rearranged the bottles behind a pile of clothes.

The next afternoon a taxi took me to the Bureau

of Health, a place swarming with seekers of health certificates, inspectors, and quasi-medical men in imposing martial uniforms. I was led to a hall where the Chief Officer was seated at an enormous table, with a world-map covering the entire wall at his back. The map was studded with coloured buttons. He addressed me straightaway, without preliminaries, 'How are you feeling?'

'In what respect?'

'Health, only health. We are not concerned with other problems you may have . . . .'

'My health is fine,' I said boastfully.

'You are from Bengal?'

'No, I am from Mysore . . . .'

'Mysore? Mysore?' he muttered, turning round to locate it on the map.

'Ah, here it is,' he pointed a baton at a patch on the map and asked, 'You notice the buttons there?'

'Yes.'

'What colour you find them?'

'Yellow,' I said, wondering if I was also being tested for colour blindness.

'Yellow indicates plague and possibly also jaundice. We get information of public health from every part of the world through the WHO reporters every hour,' he said with a glow of omniscience.

'So what?' I could not help exclaiming.

'We have to guard against carriers—especially from other Asian countries and Africa.'

'Terrible continents,' I cried.

'Glad you agree with me . . . .'

'But Mysore is a large state . . . so large that your report cannot apply to the whole state—it is bound to have sickness of some sort here and there in a village thousands of miles away from everywhere.'

'We have to go only by WHO reports.'

'One more thing. Now I am not coming from Mysore but from Coimbatore.'

'Oh! He turned his neck to locate Coimbatore—you see the purple buttons—that means malaria and cholera.'

'Is no part of this planet safe according to WHO?'

'True, true, I am glad you appreciate the situation . . . .'

I wanted to announce, 'I am not here to spread pestilence and decimate the population of the Philippines,' but suppressed it and said, 'My mission is to collect material and write a biography of your late President Magsaysay . . . .'

'Ah, he was a great leader and a wonderful commander.'

I did not want to question him whether Magsaysay was ever an army commander. I had heard of him only as the President of the country. He added, 'I was in the NMC and took direct orders from him.'

He assumed I understood what NMC meant, and I only said, 'That must have been a wonderful experience for you.'

'When I heard of his death, I went into mourning for fifteen days—even when my father died, our mourning period was only six days.'

As a result of this palaver, he showed me a

concession that although I was a risk factor carrying deadly germs around, he would not order me to be quarantined, but keep me under observation for nine days. I could stay in my hotel, but had to show myself at the bureau every afternoon and report my health.

The journey was tedious, walking every day to the health bureau and the fort. I had to sit before the Health Officer, face the world health map, answer routine questions and then return to my hotel, and stay in my room. It was not an hour safe for a stroll, as the manager had warned, 'Don't go out, down the Dwigth Way or along the beach—lot of freelance gunmen around at this hour, or taxi men who will take you downtown to places, where they will strip you of everything, including your pants.'

In support of this warning, whenever I stepped out of the hotel, a car would always come in slow gear beside me, the driver asking, 'Do you want a girl?' and taking out a photo from his pocket. 'She is a beauty, sir, who will give you anything. She is not a whore but from a respectable family, a school-teacher. If you do not like her, see this photo—or this one you may like—or this one—' He'd take out of his pocket, photo after photo. I averted my head and walked off briskly.

To digress: the streetwalkers of London accosted you, softly and seductively, whispered while you passed down Piccadilly, Curzon Street, or Soho, 'Come on, darling, let us make love—' While on a stroll with Graham Greene after dinner he would always advise, 'Don't be rude to them, just say you are not interested.'

In Rome I experienced a different kind of approach. At a restaurant table a girl would materialize and take her seat by your side, and demand, 'Give me drinks.' After that, 'I want a dinner. You want to come with me after food?'

One evening a young man kept following me while I was returning to my hotel. 'May I take you to a night club, sir? You will enjoy it, plenty of beautiful girls who will give you anything. My name is Marco, sir, why won't you let me take you to nice places?' He followed me importuning. Finally he asked, 'Why won't you let me help you to give you a good time?'

'Because my wife will be waiting for me in the hotel—she will feel lonely and upset if I don't return to the hotel.' At once he apologized, 'Excuse me, sir, if I have bothered you.'

'Not at all, Marco, you are doing your duty, nothing wrong if . . . .'

'I am glad, sir, you understand me. I don't like this profession—during the day I work hard at the Olivetti factory which is not enough for my living, so after office hours I have to work again till midnight to earn enough money—but I'll not stay like this. I am learning English and have applied for immigration and plan to go away to Canada and do farming—that's my ambition, sir.'

'Good luck to you. Be a good farmer, Marco, and good-night,' I said, when we reached my hotel.

1993

PARROTS LTD.

RAMANI RESOLVED TO BECOME A PARROT trader when he saw the following advertisement in a newspaper:

> Wanted a parrot trained to repeat the holy names of gods and slokas. Preferably in a musical manner. Prepared to pay Rs 50 to Rs 100 according to the qualification of the parrot. Communications to be addressed to . . . .

This advertisement caught his eye at a time when he was keenly searching for a congenial occupation. He considered himself to be a poet, author of *Blood-Bathed Love* and other epic efforts. He was certain that his works would be recognized by coming generations, but, at the moment, all the editors and publishers in the world stood between him and his public. Hence his search for a 'congenial' occupation. And could there be any profession more suitable to a poet than parrot trade? You lived in the haunts of parrots and spent your time in their lovely company. What an opulent life for a poet! And in this luxury there was money. 'Prepared to pay Rs 50 to Rs 100 . . . .' The fifty rupee variety was not his concern. He was not going to take the trouble to train a fourth rate parrot. He was going to trade only in the thousand-rupee variety. The Ramani stamp on a parrot was going to stand for the best in parrots and nothing less. One such parrot a month and you made your thousand a month.

He had as yet very vague notions of the parrot business but he believed in luck and intuition. Some times he sat down, pen in hand, with next to nothing in his head, and at the end of three hours the sheets of paper before him would be filled with a poetic drama or a wonderful sonnet sequence. How was it done?

Through luck and intuition. And the same qualities were now going to see him through the parrot business.

He answered the advertisement. Two days later he received a letter from one Mr Madusudhan asking him to see him at his residence in Saidapet. Ramani had no idea where parrots were available nor did he know of any parrot that could talk. All the same he had answered the advertisement in order to study the parrot market.

He inscribed on a blank visiting-card, 'T.M.T. Ramani. Managing Director, Parrots Ltd.' and started for Saidapet. He took the electric train, found his way to Madusudhan's bungalow, and sent his card in. He was ushered into a hall where a fat man, sitting cross-legged on thick piles of cushion, welcomed him. 'Ah, take that chair, Mr T.M.T. Ramani,' Madusudhan said, 'for years I have been trying to secure a decent parrot. The one I had could recite the Bhagvad Gita at dawn; but the poor creature was mauled by our neighbour's cat, and died in spite of the best medical attention. I got another one, a cockatoo from Singapore this time, beautiful colours, which used to greet visitors with "Namaste", and then would recite four stanzas of *Soundarya Lahari,* you know Shankara's inspired composition. It filled my home with holy sounds morning to night . . . .'

'Don't you like radio programmes, which start with devotional programmes every morning?'

'No, never. I abominate radio and television, and tape recorder. That is one of the reasons why my wife and children live away from me.'

'Where are they?' Ramani asked solicitously.

'Don't ask me. I am happy without them. A parrot is good enough company for me . . . .'

'What happened to the cockatoo from Singapore?'

'Some fool of a servant left the cage open one day.

It flew off, perched itself on the jack-fruit tree there, and mocked me, and fell into bad company, and then I lost sight of it. All sorts of persons promised and disappointed me. I grew desperate and advertised.'

'Ah, is that so?' Ramani asked warmly.

'I was able to get parrots that could only say, "How are you", "Ranga, Ranga", "Who is there?" and such other nonsense, but not one that could utter a prayer.'

'What a pity!' Ramani said sympathetically, 'What a pity that we didn't know each other before. We specialize in religious parrots. I am the trainer in our firm, you know.' He added as an afterthought, 'I have engaged four Brahmin priests in my department to coach the parrots.'

'Ah, how cursed am I that I did not know you before. How is it that I don't see your advertisements anywhere?'

'We don't advertise. We have our select clientele and we usually do not take up extra business.'

'How is it that I have not had the pleasure of meeting your parrots anywhere in these parts?'

'Our religious parrots sell steadily in Benares and in a few pilgrim centres in the north, but the bulk of our business is in places like South Africa.'

Ramani was offered fruits and coffee. 'I should like to see your farm sometime,' Madusudhan said.

'With pleasure,' Ramani said. 'But I am going up north for a few weeks on business. As soon as I return I will take you round our parrot farm.' He had a sudden inspiration and added, 'I have trained a few parrots in the business line too. They just quote prices and so on and are suitable for business houses. I have some for coffee houses too. These just reel off the menu. All labour-saving devices. In these days of rush and hustle they ought to be very valuable. These business-line parrots save the energy of the shop assistants who have to repeat the same thing over and over again to every customer. All the saved-up energy could be utilized by the principal of a firm for more productive purposes. This is the place of the parrot in modern economy. Would you care to see our business parrots?'

'No,' said Madusudhan. 'They aren't useful to me. I have retired from business. My thoughts are with God now. I want a bird that will be filling my house with holy sounds. I want a bird that will utter slokas. I am prepared to pay even one-thousand-four-hundred rupees for such a parrot. Please tell me when I can come for my parrot.'

'I can't say definitely when I can have one ready for you. I have some advance bookings on hand. In about two months I think I can meet your order.'

In fairness to Ramani it must be said that he had not intended to lie. He had gone there in order to understand the conditions of the parrot market but in his talk with Madusudhan his imagination caught fire and he saw Parrots Limited gradually revealed to him in all its detail of organization. It was more a loud brown study than downright falsehood.

Ramani went home and definitely made up his

mind to start the parrot business. His first transaction would be with Madusudhan. He would devote all his working hours in the next two months to training a parrot for Madusudhan. The labour would be worth Rs 1,500. In course of time, with a little practice, he could have a parrot a month ready for sale. As for customers he was confident that he could find at least one Madusudhan a month in this wide world. Certain other details of the work bothered him. Once a customer got his parrot the transaction was done with as long as the parrot lived. What was the normal longevity of a parrot? Probably ten years. So it meant that normally a customer would not return for ten years. For a moment Ramani wondered if it would be wise to earn the confidence of his customers' servants and bribe them to leave the cages open . . . .

The instinct that leads the cow to the grass and the fly to the sugar bowl was responsible for taking Ramani to Moore Market, and there one Kandan became his friend. Kandan had just been loitering around, when he noticed Ramani making eager enquiries at the stalls. He introduced himself to him: 'Master, in need of a parrot?'

'Yes.'

'What sort of a parrot?'

'A parrot that can be trained to talk. Have you one?'

'Years ago when I was in the army I had a parrot. It could give commands for the troop drill. It was our best companion at Mespot; but my officer took a fancy to it and I gave it to him . . . . I know where parrots are to be had and I can get you one if you want. . . .' In the course of an hour or two, squatting on a patch of grass in front of Moore Market and talking, a great friendship developed between Ramani and Kandan. They came to an agreement. Kandan was to secure a young parrot immediately and train it. He was to deliver the parrot fully trained in two months and receive twenty rupees in return. In due course he would be employed in Parrots Ltd. on a salary of Rs 200 a month. Before they parted for the evening a couple of rupees had changed hands.

Two days later Kandan came to Ramani's house and told him that he had purchased a young parrot from some villager. Thereafter he dropped in frequently to keep Ramani informed of the physical and mental progress of the parrot. Sometimes he demanded an odd rupee or two for buying certain secret drugs essential for the parrot's throat. In a few days he came to announce that the parrot was just able to repeat 'Krishna, Krishna' and also the first two lines of prayer to God Subramanya. Ramani was quite pleased with Kandan's work and promised to give him a bonus over the agreed amount. Even then the balance would be in his favour. He drafted the balance sheet thus:

EXPENDITURE

		Rs	A	P
Cost of parrot	:	20	0	0
Special throat drugs	:	10	0	0
Trainer's fee	:	50	0	0
Total	:	80	0	0

INCOME

		Rs	A	P
Selling price of trained parrot	:	1500	0	0
Investment	:	80	0	0
Profit	:	1420	0	0

Ramani clamoured so much to see the parrot that one dark night Kandan brought a cage with a heavy piece of cloth wrapped round it.

'I say, I can't see anything, take away the cloth,' Ramani said. 'It can't be done,' Kandan replied firmly. 'The bird is still young. It will die of paralysis if it is allowed to open its eyes on these new surroundings all of a sudden.'

'But how am I to see the bird?' Ramani asked.

'You may peep through this chink if you like.'

Ramani lifted the cage and was about to hold it against the light. 'Ah, don't do it,' Kandan screamed. 'Do you want to blind it for life?'

Ramani put down the cage. He applied his eyes to a very small opening in the cloth wrapping and said, 'I see some faint shape inside but I can't say whether it is a ball of wool or a chicken or a parrot.' At this Kandan looked so hurt that Ramani felt sorry for allowing these frivolous words to cross his lips, and apologized. Ramani asked why the bird was not fluttering its wings inside the cage. Kandan explained that he had tied its wings to its sides; otherwise there was the danger of its wasting all its energy in fluttering its wings; every ounce of its energy had to be conserved for cultivating its voice. Ramani desired to hear the voice of the parrot. Kandan declared that at night parrots could not be made to talk.

'Well, well. You may deliver it to me in working order on the thirteenth of next month.'

'No, sir, thirteen is a bad number. I'll deliver on the twelfth or the fourteenth.'

'Very well, don't delay . . . .'

'For the fourteenth definitely. It will be the most garrulous parrot one would ever wish to meet.'

'Mere garrulity is not enough,' Ramani said. 'It must be the most religious-minded parrot.'

On the fourteenth of the following month Kandan brought a green parrot in a cage. It was a rakish looking, plump bird. The sight of it sent a thrill through Ramani. He had not thought that an ambition could be so readily realized. A small thread was tied round the beak of the parrot. Kandan explained, 'It is better that you keep it tied till you reach your customer's place. Otherwise the rascal will talk all the way and gather a crowd behind you.' Ramani insisted on examining the full accomplishments of the parrot right then. Kandan requested Ramani to go out of the room for a few minutes and he would untie the thread and coax the bird. Of course it could be made to talk even in Ramani's presence but then it might take time, and he (Kandan) had to go and attend on his aunt, who was lying in a serious condition in the General Hospital. He could coax the bird much quicker if Ramani would oblige him by going out. Ramani went out of the room. Presently he heard the gruff voice of Kandan coaxing the bird.

And then the parrot uttered in a melodious voice 'Krishna, Krishna', 'Rama, Rama', and the first two lines of a prayer to God Subramanya. 'As soon as you take him over to your customer's place snip off the thread with scissors. If you give him a red, ripe chilli he will be very friendly with you in an hour or two, and then you can coax him to utter the holy sounds.'

'Right, thanks. Do you want your money now?'

'Hm, yes,' said Kandan. 'I have to buy some medicines for my aunt.'

Ramani took his savings bank-book, went to the Vepery Post Office, bled his account white, and handed fifty rupees to Kandan. The old clerk at the counter looked at Ramani sourly. He looked on Ramani's recent withdrawals with marked disfavour. Ramani said apologetically, 'I will come back in the evening and deposit a thousand rupees.'

Kandan took leave of Ramani and hurried away to his aunt's bedside.

'Ah ! Ah ! Come in, Mr Ramani,' said Madusudhan as soon as Ramani appeared in Saidapet with a parrot in hand. 'I am so happy that you have brought the parrot. Really! Really! Or am I dreaming? Ah, you are correct to the hour.'

'In business, punctuality is everything,' said Ramani. Madusudhan took him in. He inspected the cage with delight; and asked again and again if the holy names of gods were going to echo through his halls thenceforth. 'Does the bird really utter the names of Krishna and Rama?'

'Absolutely,' Ramani replied. 'It was trained under my personal supervision.'

They sat on a sofa with the cage between them. Ramani took a pair of scissors and snipped off the thread tied round the beak. He took out a ripe chilli and gave it to the bird. It ate the chilli gratefully.

Ramani said, 'Since this is a new place it will take about half an hour for him to open his mouth.'

'Let him. Let him take his own time,' said Madusudhan. Ramani thrust another chilli into the cage and the parrot attacked it with vigour. They watched it for sometime, and then Madusudhan asked, 'Will you have your cheque immediately or sometime later?'

Ramani was not used to such questions. He grinned awkwardly and said, 'Oh, I have not brought the receipt book.'

'It does not matter. You can send the receipt later on.'

'May we hope for another order from you?'

It was at this stage that the shrieking question was asked in Tamil, 'Are you drunk or mad?' It was followed by the command, 'Get out, you fool!' Ramani looked at the cage in consternation. The parrot had eaten all the chilli and was now in a loquacious mood. He chuckled quietly, and winked at Ramani before saying in lucid English, 'Hands up or I shoot! You son of a . . . .' Madusudhan choked as he asked, 'Are these the holy sounds that are going to fill my house?' He glared at Ramani.

'There is some mistake,' mumbled Ramani. He suddenly rose and fled, leaving the cage behind. He did not stop to turn and look till he reached his house in Vepery.

Two days later a small advertisement in a paper said:

> LOST: a green parrot in cage kept in the front veranda. Finder will be rewarded . . . .

Ramani wondered for a moment if it would be worth his while to put this person on the track of the parrot. But he realized that he might be hauled up for theft. For sometime he lived in terror of being hunted down by Madusudhan, but fortunately the visiting-card he had left behind contained only his name and not his address.

MAN-HUNT

THE NEWSPAPER ADVERTISEMENT PRESENTED the photo of a young man (with a porcupine-quill crop, a wide mouth, and dot- like eyes) and said:

> A reward of hundred rupees will be given to anyone who helps me to find my son, E.D. Gopalkrishnan missing from home since last Thursday.

And then followed a few lines giving the age, colour, and height of this lost soul.

Sankar pondered over this advertisement and apostrophized:

'I don't know why you want to throw away good money and get this son back; but it is none of my business. What I want to know is if you will part with your money irrespective of whether the lad is produced before you dead or alive. You see, I may pick him up from the sea, or suppose it is impossible to bring him over unless you stun him first?'

Madras being a big city it was possible that a man might chance on a missing son. If one was in luck that was how money came one's way. And this quest would not involve any extra work for Sankar since already he wandered a great deal every day seeing managers, superintendents, and bosses, in the hope of securing employment; all that he would have to do now would be to keep a watchful eye on fellow-passengers in trams and on the passers-by in the streets.

Sankar had come down to Madras six months before from Tanjore, having failed to find anything worthwhile to do in his birthplace. He lived with some relations in a backstreet in Triplicane. Every morning he left home at ten and returned only at eight in the evening, spending the interval mostly in trams for which he had a cheap, monthly ticket.

He needed the hundred rupees in order to try a favourite scheme of his. He believed that there was a vast, unexploited market for lime and mango pickles in the kitchens of the European folk in India. One needed capital to buy mangoes, limes and spices, and to grease the palms of the butlers, who ruled over the European kitchens. On the horizon of this vision there were cases of pickles waiting on the wharf to be shipped to America.

That day as he sat in the tram going to Broadway, Sankar subjected every in-coming face to a thorough scrutiny. He staggered up and down the tram in order to look at two persons sitting with their backs to him. There were less than a dozen passengers—a couple of women and some middle-aged men, not one bearing even a remote resemblance to the photo in the paper. All the same Sankar performed his duty religiously, by pulling the newspaper cutting out of his pocket and comparing the faces about him with the face in the paper.

Before evening he had travelled in a score of trams, tramped most of the important thoroughfares in George Town, been into almost every public building from the High Court down to free reading rooms, watched the doorways of ten coffee hotels, pulled the newspaper cutting out of his pocket a hundred times and gazed intently on a thousand faces. His last spot for the day was the beach where a vast crowd sat around the radio stand enjoying the music. At seven-thirty he suddenly realized that he had been working continuously for nine hours. His head ached from eye-strain, and he was foot-sore. He turned homeward.

Next morning he planned for the day: he would comb the hospitals, rest-houses, museum, and the harbour, and also if possible, keep an eye on the ticket windows at theatres.

While walking along the litter-covered,

spit-stained footpath in Esplanade, Providence brought him face to face with his quarry, who was descending the steps of the restaurant in the YMCA building. Sankar stepped aside, with his heart palpitating. When he recovered from the excitement he pulled out the photo: ah, there was no mistaking: it seemed as though the photo had become animated and was walking before him. He thrust the photo back in his pocket and ran after the other who was moving towards China Bazaar. Sankar caught up with him, touched his elbow and panted, 'Can you direct me to Mowbray's Road?'

'I don't know where it is. I am also new to the place.' He turned to go. Sankar held him by the arm.

'Why do you hold my arm?'

'Forgive me,' Sankar said, 'I feel so nervous in this city that I want to hold onto someone. Will you let me walk with you?'

Sankar's mind was troubled by a few doubts as he kept pace with the other: he appeared to be more than seventeen; over five feet in height, and not very dark. On every side he seemed to overflow the frame set for him by the specifications in the advertisement. But Sankar consoled himself: 'The advertiser could not have weighed, measured, and tested the boy before he stepped out of the house.'

'My name is Sankar,' he announced above the screech of tram wheels, and asked, 'What is yours?'

'Why do you want it?' asked the other suspiciously, having, like a true country cousin, heard all about the pimps, pickpockets, and confidence-men of Madras.

'Just to know, that is all,' said Sankar, 'I feel so relieved to meet a friendly face. You needn't tell me if you don't want to.'

'My name is Tirumalai,' said the other, and Sankar's heart sank because the name in the advertisement was 'Gopalkrishnan'. He was unhappy for a moment. But he suddenly realized that he was a fool to have expected the other to give out his real name. He too in the other's position would call himself 'Tirumalai', 'Micky Mouse', or anything that came to his head.

'Where exactly are you going?' Sankar asked ingratiatingly, a hundred yards further.

'What do you care where I go?' said the other without turning.

'I want to know because I am also going there.'

'Don't pester me. Go away.'

'Listen to this. I am afraid of everything here. I am not asking for anything impossible. Just let me see the places with you. I don't want money or anything. I only want your friendship and company. Don't fear that when you go to a hotel you may have to feed me. I will wait for you at the hotel door while you are eating.'

Tirumalai didn't reply. He walked on. He walked rather fast, Sankar had almost to trot behind him. He felt humiliated and asked rather curtly, 'Are you deaf ? Didn't you hear what I said?'

Tirumalai turned his head, shook his fist, and said, 'If you don't leave me alone I will call a policeman,' and marched forward.

Police: That settled it. A few minutes later, Sankar suddenly commanded, 'Stop!' The other, taken aback by the tone, obeyed.

Sankar gripped his arm, scowled at him and whispered, 'Idiot! Call a policeman and see what happens.' He tightened his grip and added, 'Come quietly with me. I have got to find out a few things about you. I will let you go when I have done my business with you. I know something about you. After the recent bank raid we have been more watchful than you fools imagine.'

'What have I done?'

'Nothing, I hope. All the same I have to ask you one or two questions. If you come without any fuss it will be for your own good. Otherwise you will find yourself in a lock-up.'

Hand in hand, friends to all appearance, they walked down the road. Whenever he glanced at the other, Sankar felt like crooning: 'Oh, you lovely one, my hundred rupees in flesh and blood!' while his mind conjured up visions of pickles, butlers and shipping cases.

Now after securing the young man he was at a loss to know what to do with him. He made him walk all the way to a park. They sat under a tree. Sankar said suddenly, 'I want you to give me about twelve annas. It will be returned to you. I want to send a wire to Jalarpet. Isn't that your place?'

'Yes, how did you know?'

'I have to send a message about you. The earlier we do it the better for you. I haven't any change with me. If you haven't any with you either, I am afraid, we have to go back to Flower Bazaar Police Station for it. I thought you might not like it.'

As they walked, hand in hand again, to the Choolai Post Office, Sankar said with a chuckle, 'Your father will come and take you back home tomorrow.'

'Indeed! Why?'

'Well, one has to go back home, you know.'

'I left home only last evening.'

'No,' said Sankar, 'much earlier than that. Now that we are about it, don't you think you are too old to run away from home? You could as well have taken leave of everybody and told them where you were going.'

The other suddenly sat down on the road, beat his head with his hands and said, 'Siva! Siva! I now understand. I am also here in search of him.' Sankar's heart felt the first stab of doubt, but only for a brief second. He said with a cynical laugh, 'Of course that is what I too would say in your place.'

He pulled out of his pocket the newspaper photo and asked, 'Who is this?'

The other started a little at the sight of it, and said, 'Oh, of course it is me, ah!' He opened his mouth to say something, swallowed his words, looked suddenly cheerful and said, 'All right. I give myself up. You may wire to my father.'

Sankar was puzzled by this change: 'What makes you so happy?'

'Nothing, nothing. The thought of home perhaps—'

The next morning they were at the Central Station when the Bangalore Mail arrived. Tirumalai peered into the compartments, and hailed an old man.

Sankar asked, 'Are you very nervous to meet your father?'

The old man came up and exclaimed eagerly. 'So after all!' The reunion lacked the excitement and drama that Sankar had expected of it. The old man looked at Tirumalai without enthusiasm and asked, 'Where is Gopalkrishnan?'

'Siva alone knows.'

'Do you mean to say that Gopalkrishnan is not here?'

'Yes, I think I mean it,' said Tirumalai.

'Then why, why the telegram?' asked the old man.

'How can I say? Ask this gentleman, who is in the police, why the telegram was sent. He did it, perhaps because he found the lost person according to the photo in the newspaper.'

'But were you a dumb animal not to have told him?'

'What is the matter? Why all this commotion?' asked Sankar.

'This is the matter, sir,' said the old man. 'My sight is not what it used to be, and so I suppose the wrong photo went to the paper. When I tell the paper fellows that they have printed the wrong photo they demand money again to print the right one. I ask you, is it just? Is it reasonable?'

'But this is your son, isn't he?'

'Ah, isn't he? So is another, and another, and

another. It is the last one that is gone. I sent this rascal here to look for him and he is playing all kinds of tricks on an old man.'

The son said, 'It would have cost you less if you had listened to people and not grudged a little money to have the right photo printed.'

'Don't try to advise your elders; you mind your business.'

Sankar muttered, 'I have stepped into a nest of lunatics.' He wondered for a moment whether he should stick to the matter of the offer in the advertisement and demand the reward. But he felt too weary and fatigued to haggle. He told the old man, 'You owe this person twelve annas; don't fail to pay it to him,' and abruptly walked out of the platform.

READ MORE IN PENGUIN

In every corner of the world, on every subject under the sun, Penguin represents quality and variety—the very best in publishing today.

For complete information about books available from Penguin—including Puffins, Penguin Classics and Arkana—and how to order them, write to us at the appropriate address below. Please note that for copyright reasons the selection of books varies from country to country.

In India: Please write to *Penguin Books India Pvt. Ltd. 11 Community Centre, Panchsheel Park, New Delhi 110017*

In the United Kingdom: Please write to *Dept JC, Penguin Books Ltd. Bath Road, Harmondsworth, West Drayton, Middlesex, UB7 ODA. UK*

In the United States: Please write to *Penguin Putnam Inc., 375 Hudson Street, New York, NY 10014*

In Canada: Please write to *Penguin Books Canada Ltd. 10 Alcorn Avenue, Suite 300, Toronto, Ontario M4V 3B2*

In Australia: Please write to *Penguin Books Australia Ltd. 487, Maroondah Highway, Ring Wood, Victoria 3134*

In New Zealand: Please write to *Penguin Books (NZ) Ltd. Private Bag, Takapuna, Auckland 9*

In the Netherlands: Please write to *Penguin Books Netherlands B.V., Keizersgracht 231 NL-1016 DV Amsterdom*

In Germany : Please write to *Penguin Books Deutschland GmbH, Metzlerstrasse 26, 60595 Frankfurt am Main, Germany*

In Spain: Please write to *Penguin Books S.A., Bravo Murillo, 19-1'B, E-28015 Madrid, Spain*

In Italy: Please write to *Penguin Italia s.r.l., Via Felice Casati 20, I-20104 Milano*

In France: Please write to *Penguin France S.A., 17 rue Lejeune, F-31000 Toulouse*

In Japan: Please write to *Penguin Books Japan. Ishikiribashi Building, 2-5-4, Suido, Tokyo 112*

In Greece: Please write to *Penguin Hellas Ltd, dimocritou 3, GR-106 71 Athens*

In South Africa: Please write to *Longman Penguin Books Southern Africa (Pty) Ltd, Private Bag X08, Bertsham 2013*

A WRITER'S NIGHTMARE

R.K. Narayan

R.K. Narayan, perhaps India's best-known living writer, is better known as a novelist but his essays are as delightful and enchanting as his stories and novels. *A Writer's Nightmare* includes essays on subjects as diverse as weddings, higher mathematics, South Indian coffee, umbrellas, monkeys, the caste system—all sorts of topics, simple and not so simple, which reveal the very essence of India.

'(A book) to be dipped into and savoured'
— *Sunday*